D1538228

Love in black & white

Photographs and Interviews by Mary Motley Kalergis

Love in black & white

Photographs and Interviews by Mary Motley Kalergis

Foreword by Julius Lester

Dafina
BOOKS

CONTENTS

FOREWORD

The concept of race is a social and political construct that assigns values to biologically neutral markers of skin color, hair texture, facial features, etc. Studies conducted by The Human Genome Project tell us that 99.9 percent of the DNA of every person on earth is identical. Anthropologists have concluded that everyone who has ever lived and will live is descended from a common African ancestor. "Human beings are so similar that it makes no difference biologically for a white to marry a black, or an Asian to marry an Australian. More intermarriage will make it harder to figure out an individual's ancestry. But it can only hasten the approach of a color-blind society." ("The Genetic Archaeology of Race," by Steve Olson, *The Atlantic Monthly*, April 2001.)

In the not too distant future, our descendants will look back and scratch their heads in perplexity that there was a time when people formed opinions, made laws and social policy, and acted with disrespect and contempt toward others solely on the basis of skin color. Although slavery and racial segregation have ended, the thinking and attitudes that produced them cannot be expunged by pieces of legislation. Ideas and attitudes change one person at a time.

That's why it is important to look at the faces so beautifully photographed by Mary Motley Kalergis. At first one might notice and be startled by the contrasting blackness and whiteness of the people portrayed but almost immediately the difference in their races becomes secondary to the obvious love each couple shares. In their faces we experience the beauty that love and love alone makes of us all.

In their words we hear them reflect on themselves as sociological pioneers helping to create a society in which race is divested of value and meaning. Listen.

"If folks can hold on to the idea that we're all individuals, instead of 'you people' or 'those people,' there would be less suspicion and more respect. Society and history is made up of many individual stories." (Bozz Bosley)

"Racism is a contagion of insanity. One generation passes it on to the next. Martha and I have made a family that stops the insanity. Our kids don't have anything invested in identifying with being black or white." (Larry Meyers)

"We need to revolutionize our perceptions of ourselves and each other." (Veronica Williams)

"My parents have told me that they've learned so much from seeing the two of us together, what's important and what's not." (Suzanne Jones)

What's important? What's not important? That is the question. These couples tell us that love is important. If you think race is what's important, you might miss out on love.

The presence of couples such as these in cities and small towns across the nation indicate that America is changing, that America is beginning to fulfill its human promise. America is the only country in history whose population is comprised of people from every part of the globe. This country is attempting to do what has never been done in world history, namely, create a homogenous nation from the lives and cultures of people from every continent. This is an extraordinary and brave undertaking that seeks to turn the rhetoric of the oneness of the human family into a reality. Prof. Luigi Luca Cavalli-Sforza, a professor of genetics at Stanford University, posits what he calls "the American model". "Two hundred years from now people all over the world will be mixing in the same way that people in the United States are today." ("The Genetic Archaeology of Race," by Steve Olson, *The Atlantic Monthly*, April 2001.)

In these pages are images and words of an America in the process of fulfilling its human potential as a nation, a nation in which people are learning what's important and what's not.

Julius Lester
University of Massachusetts/Amherst

INTRODUCTION

1 was a young girl in the late 1950s and early 1960s when news coverage of the Civil Rights Movement first inspired me to become a photographer. The black and white photographs of the freedom marches and sit-ins, and of those brave people facing fire hoses and police dogs as they fought for their rights as Americans, made an indelible impression on me. As a child of that era, *Life* magazine taught me about the ongoing struggle to secure the innate dignity of the individual, and the power of photography to drive that message home. Martin Luther King's ringing affirmations of freedom had the same influence on me that the speeches of Franklin Roosevelt or Winston Churchill must have had on my parents' generation during the dark years of the Second World War. However, I never thought, as a white southerner who grew up cradled within the domestic privileges of Virginia apartheid, the topic of race was mine to take on as an author.

But in 1997, I published a book entitled *With This Ring: A Portrait of Marriage*. A white friend of mine, who's married to a black man, suggested that my next book be about interracial couples. My first reaction was that I had already done a book about couples and commitment, and that love transcends race. The national uproars surrounding the Rodney King video tape and the O.J. Simpson murder trial, however, were vivid reminders to me that this country still had a long way to go before blacks and whites share the same American experience.

The premise of this book is simple: if we honestly want to examine race relations in America, who better to observe than interracial couples, whose lives form a unique bridge between black and white cultures? Biracial families teach us from firsthand experience about the invisible caste system that haunts our national consciousness. This examination of black and white romance offers an intensely personal perspective on one of our most challenging national questions—can our society move beyond the resentment, guilt, and expectations that are the legacy of slavery and segregation?

It wasn't until the landmark Loving vs. Virginia decision in 1967 that the anti-miscegenation laws were overturned by the U.S. Supreme Court, but societal attitudes change even more slowly than law. Although integration of schools and the workplace has removed many of the barriers between the races, apprehension over interracial dating and marriage continues. While most parents now accept that their children's neighbors, classmates, and co-workers may be of different races, many are terrified to contemplate that their own grandchildren may be a different color.

I see the walls of segregation slowly crumbling, one couple at a time. The results often have a positive ripple effect on family, friends, neighbors, and co-workers, because biracial children from mixed marriages blur the final boundaries of segregation. But even though Tiger Woods calls himself a "Cablinasian" (referring to his Caucasian, Black, Indian, and Asian heritage), he still might have trouble hailing a cab at night. When passion scales the walls of racism, the results threaten our society's basic unspoken assumptions of acceptability. Look at the resistance of scholars to contemplate the possibility that the widowed Thomas Jefferson fathered the children of his slave and deceased wife's half-sister, Sally Hemings (whose mother was the slave of his father-in-law.) The couples in these pages dare to challenge those assumptions of acceptability that still exist today. These families are the pioneers of the ultimate act of integration, and this book bears witness to their individual stories.

To me, the most compelling communication is the individual story. Documentary photography focuses directly on the human condition through the unblinking gaze of a camera. When coupled with the personal interview, a life is revealed, softening our innate distrust of strangers or "those people". The couples in *Love in Black and White* are visible proof that racial harmony can be achieved, and the radiant faces of their children are a living reproach to the ignorance of bigotry.

Mary Motley Kalergis

Michael has an innocence about him that is a strength rather than a weakness, and I was quite taken by his caring enthusiasm. My parents were immediately fond of him as well, and Michael's race was never an issue. But my mum hated the idea of me leaving England to live in the States. Emigrating to America and dealing with all the associated changes was the biggest hurdle to overcome in the first few years of our marriage. For me, it was very important that I not lose my identity. I must admit that early in our marriage, I was unprepared for some of the looks we'd get when Michael and I were together. I suppose I was completely naive, but I honestly didn't give the difference in our race much thought. I have never seen a color when I look at Michael."

"My concern has always been with what I feel is right, rather than what other people might think. I always choose to give people the benefit of the doubt. So if people stare at us, I assume it's because Judith is a beautiful woman, not because they are uncomfortable with an interracial couple. When I was in England I felt very much at home. It seemed natural for us to become a couple. There wasn't much struggle involved. When I had to leave Judith behind and return to the United States, I realized that our separation was an unnatural state, and that we belonged together."

"When he presented me with an engagement ring, it threw me for a loop. I was so happy, yet I realized that my life was going to undergo some pretty drastic changes. As soon as I graduated from medical school, Michael returned to England for our wedding. Two months later I made the trip to the States, even though I knew I wouldn't be able to practice medicine here. I began working in medical research and found the work extremely stimulating; as a result I'm currently pursuing a doctoral degree in molecular medicine. I won't say the transition wasn't sometimes difficult after I left England, but I can honestly say that I have no regrets."

"When I look back, I'm amazed by the twists and turns in my life— the complete unpredictability of the road. My mom was a housekeeper for Peter Weeks, the headmaster at St. Anne's Belfield School. I received a scholarship to attend the school, and then, when our house burned down, the Weeks family took me into their home to live. Now I both teach and coach at St. Anne's, in addition to being director for Alumni Affairs; so I feel as though I have come a long way, without going very far! While I was in England, the Weeks family sent my mother over for a visit and I'll never forget the sense of wonder we both had being there together."*

"I think Michael gets a lot of his initiative and courage from his mother; I really admire her. She has a strength of spirit that shines through. Michael always sees the good in people and he is very trusting; I'm really drawn to that quality in him. I've definitely mellowed under his influence..."

"My mother never let us stray too far from her vision of people, which was

> *"We already know it's a boy and my role as his father is to teach him to be a decent man, whose values transcend race."*

that, regardless of color, people are basically good. Working for the Weeks family, she got to know white people up close, just as I did, both by living with their family, and going to St. Anne's. Once you get to know people, you quickly learn that we have many more similarities than differences. I remember Ruth Weeks touching my hair, which was braided at the time, because she was curious about its texture. Knowledge breaks down fear of the unknown. Occasionally, when things get difficult, and I feel under pressure, I'll drive out the old dirt road where I grew up and think about what really matters. I find I can't feel sorry for myself for very long. I eagerly anticipate the birth of our unborn child. We already know it's a boy and my role as his father is to teach him to be a decent man, whose values transcend race. I hope to teach him the value of hard work and to stand for things that are important to people of all races. Making a difference is what really matters.

We were both working as nurse's aids in a Massachusetts hospital when we first met," says James, in his rich southern accent. "One day she asked me for a ride home and it just went from there. I was raised up in Virginia during a time when you weren't supposed to cross the color line, but I've never been one who was afraid to cross a line. They didn't integrate the schools in Southampton County until my senior year in high school. But when they did, I just got on the bus and never looked back. My own children have a hard time realizing what life was like back then, and I think that's basically a good thing. The lingering resentments of both races are finally starting to clear up with our kids' generation, because they have no memory of how little opportunity blacks had back in the old days."

"The first thing I noticed about James when I first saw him was that he was a nice looking man. His sense of humor really got my attention. He's always telling me I don't notice stuff, and I think that's probably true, because I really didn't focus on his southern accent or the color of his skin," says Patricia in her own New England accent, mellowed by the years of living in rural Virginia.

"It touched me how she asked me to give her a ride home from work, without the slightest hint of nervousness. As a black man, you get used to people treating you with suspicion, so I was quite taken with her trust. A naive heart is a non-judgmental heart, and I was struck by that rare quality."

"Growing up where I did, there were very few blacks around for me to get to know, though I would sometimes baby-sit for the one black family in the neighborhood. I certainly never dated anyone outside of my race before I met James. My parents were concerned that people might give us a hard time as a couple, but they [her parents] never gave us a hard time. They liked James."

"It was hard on Patty to leave her family and come to Virginia, but when my mama started to get old and sick, I just had to come back home. My mother was very concerned about the two of us moving to Southampton County, because it's a place with a long history of segregation. In her day it would have been unthinkable for a mixed couple to live together."

"We've been here twelve years now. There's still very few mixed families in this part of Virginia, and even though I've seen white girls shipped out of the county to boarding school when they start dating a black classmate, I haven't felt much prejudice against James and I as a couple. Maybe that's because I am from outside the community."

"You've got to remember, that in the South, white and black have always lived around each other, so in a strange way, it's not so uncomfortable for folks to see us together. No matter what race you are, we're all put here on this earth for the same reason—to survive, grow, and prosper. Human nature is the same for all people everywhere. It all comes

> "Man is a much more primitive being than we like to acknowledge. We're fearful of that truth, so we're filled with irrational prejudices."

down to sex. Man is a much more primitive being than we like to acknowledge. We're fearful of that truth, so we're filled with irrational prejudices. In this country, we're totally obsessed with sex at the same time that we try to deny the power of its existence. Sex is the pathway to life. There's definitely a lingering invisible color line in America. We're not supposed to talk about it, but it's there. It has to do with sex. When a black man gets with a white woman, some folks look at that as a way for the black man to get even for the way he's been mistreated through the years. If I was trying to get even, I'd have a harem—I wouldn't stop with one! They'd have to get the Klan on my case for sure. But, if I was about revenge, I wouldn't have married at all. I'd just get even. Being a hardworking husband and father is certainly not very vengeful."

n high school," says Tony, "I felt like I didn't fit in anywhere. The black kids thought I acted too white and the white kids thought I was too black. I felt like an outsider everywhere. I tried to fit in with the other black kids by changing my haircut and clothes and talking slang, but I felt like an imposter instead of myself."

"We really had different school experiences, because I never got good grades and was always getting in trouble. My friends were mostly black, because I was attracted to the dope selling 'gangsta' life. I guess I thought it was cool and it made me feel good that they accepted me," recalls Sean.

"He was always kind to me, and I was attracted to the fact that behind his rough exterior, Sean was really sweet. And even though he was white, he was totally accepted by the black crowd, which was something I wasn't successful at, and that probably made Sean even more desirable to me."

"She seemed like such an upstanding person, I couldn't dare believe there was any way that we could be together."

"I might be book smart, but my husband is really mechanically inclined. If something's broken, he can pretty much always fix it. When I started going to the university, I finally found a group of black kids that dressed and talked like me, but at the same time, they were less tolerant about interracial dating than the high school students. I'd get invitations to things by other black students and they'd say, 'Maybe you shouldn't bring Sean.'"

"I wasn't aware of the black students' racism towards me as much as I figured they were kind of snobby because they were college students and they looked at me as a local."

"When I got pregnant my second year in college, my black friends there said, 'Don't have that white boy's baby.' There was no way I could have an abortion. We'd already decided that we'd get married and have kids one day, so when I got pregnant, the only change was the timing.

I always equated sex with love and love with marriage and marriage with children. That's one of the reasons I loved Sean in the first place, because I knew he was that kind of person."

"I was raised without a father and I always swore that I'd never do that to my children. I think becoming a father has been the best thing in the world for me. I've felt a lot calmer on the inside ever since."

"My father was dead set against us being together at first, but now that he sees Sean as my husband and the father of his grandchildren, there's nothing he wouldn't do for him. Since we've been married, most of our close friends are other biracial couples. It's nice for both of us to finally have a circle of friends where we feel we really belong."

"All you ever hear about is the bad news. If there's a terrible racist

> "All you ever hear about is the bad news. You don't hear about couples like Tony and me. I get up and go to work, while she takes care of the kids. I guess there's no headlines in that."

act, like that poor black guy that was dragged behind a pickup truck in Texas, it gets on the six o'clock news. But you don't hear much about couples like Tony and me. I get up and go to work, while she takes care of the kids. I guess there are no headlines in that. But if you think about it, that's a shame, because that's important stuff. I guess we're quite the odd couple, with me dropping out of high school while she's got her degree at one of the best universities in the country. It goes to show that you just shouldn't stereotype."

A friend from work suggested that we meet. When we got together for drinks, I remembered having met Craig years before at a party, and he had a funky, downtown air about him. This time he looked more 'uptown' in his corporate suit and Armani tie, and I remember thinking that the combination of funky and corporate was great."

"It wasn't a very auspicious start for me. I was still recovering from a bad breakup, and the first thing I noticed about Marty was these horrific white shoes. Frankly, the whiteness of her skin wasn't an issue at all, but, man, those shoes were a serious obstacle to overcome!"

"With Craig, taste was more an issue than race. We're both architects, so we have strong ideas about matters of aesthetics. Once he got over my shoes—which by the way I still love!—we discovered that we had a lot in common: we came from similar backgrounds, went to similar schools. While we were dating there wasn't any tension because we were an interracial couple, although I do recall one friend telling me he thought I was 'awfully brave' to marry a black man."

"When we told our parents that we were getting married, they seemed genuinely pleased. Race wasn't an uncomfortable issue for my family. They had the same set of social and political values as Marty's parents. I grew up in a predominantly white neighborhood and even though I was too young to remember the event, my parents were apparently courageous pioneers, moving out of the black section of town. As they were preparing to purchase their house, the neighborhood held an ad hoc meeting to figure out a way to prevent my parents from moving in. My father stood up in an extremely vitriolic meeting and explained how he wanted the same thing for his children they wanted for theirs. He actually persuaded them to do the right thing."

"There's a big difference in experiences from one generation to the next. Certainly Craig and I haven't had to deal with any hostile groups trying to keep us out of the neighborhood. Our parents get along better than most in-laws: both sets actually spend many holidays all together with us."

"Living in New York City can pretty much insulate you from the indignities of racism. Of course, they're all the more stinging when you are confronted,
because it's more unexpected. I don't care if I am wearing an expensive suit, I've had plenty of on-duty cabs pass me by."*

"I had never, ever had that happen to me until I was standing next to my husband. It was an important moment for me the first time it happened, because it opened my eyes to the fact that black people aren't as paranoid about racism as whites tend to think they are."

"Remember that very WASPy lady on the ferry to Nantucket, who saw I was wearing a Brown sweatshirt and asked if I knew someone who went to Brown?" recalls Craig.

"Right . That was early in our relationship, and when I saw that Craig was insulted it took me some time to realize why—that she assumed that because he was black he probably hadn't gone to an Ivy League school himself. Now I am

> "Black Americans are suspicious because they are treated differently—it's not just in their imagination. That's where the misunderstanding between black and white lies, because most white people aren't privy to the subtle indignities that haunt blacks in their daily lives."

quicker to perceive this subtle kind of prejudice. I was less amazed by the outcome of the O.J. Simpson trial than many whites, for instance. I understood how the O.J. jury could have honestly perceived reasonable doubt. For blacks it isn't much of a stretch to believe that there was police harassment involved. Black Americans are suspicious because they are treated differently—it's not just in their imagination. That's where the misunderstanding between black and white lies, because most white people

aren't privy to the subtle indignities that haunt blacks every day. When black people say, 'It's a black thing, you wouldn't understand,' I get it now. For me, marrying Craig opened up this whole world of experience, whereas he has continued to live as he had been, as a black man in a predominantly white world. I think he's expanded my world more than the other way around."

"I know about white culture and society. I've functioned successfully in it my whole life, but most white folks don't have a clue what it's like to be black in this country. By marrying a white woman, my ability to be indignant about things is in some ways tempered by my understanding of white values, though there's not enough money to completely buy yourself out of the problem of racism. New York was unusual in that anything goes out on the street, in public,

but there certainly were buildings and neighborhoods that actively excluded people of color. I remember after we had our first baby, and we were looking for a bigger place, we found a great place in Brooklyn. The landlord didn't want kids, we were told, which was pretty suspect since there were strollers all over the place."

"We ended up buying a house in an old Italian neighborhood, and we loved it there, and never felt anything but embraced by the neighbors and business people."

"It's fascinating to me that, as a black man in an interracial marriage, living in the South isn't at all uncomfortable for me. Southern whites have always crossed paths with blacks on a daily basis, so you don't feel so alien as you

might in a white community up north."

"He was really nervous about moving to the South, and the interesting thing is that we know more interracial couples here and have more black friends than we did in New York City. Blacks and whites seem to actually interact more easily here, and without the overriding sense of fear that you find on the street and in the subways in New York City."

"...especially among the working class," continues Craig. "One of the first things I noticed here was that the black and white sanitation workers ride on the same trucks, working side by side. You would never see that in New York. I can hardly think of an instance where Marty and I have been treated badly because of our different races..."

"...or our children either..." adds Marty.

"There's a certain level of civility in the middle class, academic environment we inhabit that precludes any name calling or overt rudeness, but there are daily subtleties, like someone avoiding touching your hand when they make change, or having to show an absurd amount of identification when you write a check. People have said to us, 'Oh, you're so brave sending your kids to the city schools, it's so...diverse.' What they're saying in their own polite way is, 'There are so many black

kids there.' Our three kids haven't felt much pressure to take a stand on their racial and ethnic diversity, though I suspect it will be an issue for them at some point."

"Right now in our house there is a fluidity about issues of race and color.

"What I really hope for is for our kids not to have to choose between black and white, for a world which accepts them for who they are, which we think is the best of both worlds."

The kids are clear whose skin is what color, and whose hair is relatively curly or straight, but it doesn't necessarily correlate with being 'African American' or 'White.' What I really hope for is for our kids not to have to choose between black and white, for a world which accepts them for who they are, which we think is the best of both worlds."

1 grew up in a big white house in a Boston suburb and went to a private girls' school, where I played field hockey and lacrosse. There was absolutely no diversity in my school or my neighborhood. My environment was pretty much filled with blue-eyed blondes until I went to college in Maine. My dad was a doctor and my mom, a nurse."

"I always went to Charlottesville public schools," says Boyd. "My dad was a custodial worker for the school system and my mom, a maid. Even though they didn't go to college, they were proud that I did, though I was never pressured to do so. My father was a choir director in church and my grandfather used to play 'Joy to the World' on the accordion, so my family is probably directly responsible for my love of music. In sixth grade I wanted to learn how to play the guitar, so I signed up for a stringed instrument class. Of course, there were no guitars involved in the class, so I gave the violin a try and immediately fell in love with the instrument. In high school, I was a good student and involved in a lot of extra-curricular activities, like drama and student government, and I think some of the other black students thought I wasn't quite 'down'. If you're black and smart in school, you do have to show a little bit of extra toughness to survive that. When I was a teenager, standing out for being a bit different sometimes made things difficult, but it pays off in the long run, because it builds character."

"That's one thing Boyd's got plenty of—character! How we met is really a kind of interesting story. A friend of mine insisted that I go hear him play music, because she was convinced that I'd fall for him in a big way. I have no idea why, because she didn't know me very well and she didn't know Boyd at all. When she finally dragged me to hear him, I literally gasped out loud. He took my breath away. His music and his smile just knocked me out. I'd never felt so immediately attracted to anyone before. I kept saying, 'Your eyes are amazing,' and he kept saying, 'Your legs, your legs!'"

"The guys in the band were observing the whole thing. There's not much privacy in a band. That was about ten years ago and we've been together ever since. From early on, our relationship was unusual. At the very beginning, we'd talk about what our child would look like and discuss possible names."

"It was so romantic when we got engaged. He totally surprised me with this beautiful ring. I kept waking up in the night and looking at my finger, thinking, 'Oh my God—I'm engaged to get married. What are my parents going to say?' I was nervous when I first met his parents, because I didn't think this blond-haired field hockey player was their idea of an ideal daughter-in-law, but they were wonderfully welcoming to me. My own parents had a little more trouble getting used to us as a couple, but pretty soon they became crazy about Boyd. They were

> "I think our daughter Abby is lucky because she gets to experience the richness of both black and white culture, which is a wonderful kind of cultural fusion that all Americans should share."

more concerned over the fact that he was a musician than the color of his skin. They strongly believed in a college degree and a 'conventional job' and they used to put a lot of pressure on me to put pressure on Boyd to give up his dream."

"I'd dropped out of the university because I just didn't want to be there. All I could think about was my music."

"When I look back at the pressure I was putting on him to stay in school, I kick myself. Up until about a year ago, I think my parents were still hoping Boyd would get a 'real job' instead of being a musician. Now they're just tremendously respectful of his accomplishments."

"I always had gigs. I've always been fortunate to have my music support me. I knew from the first time I played with Dave Matthews that the musicians and songs were right and that we really had something to work with. The whole process of playing for thirty people in the windowsill of a restaurant, with Ricardo just having a snare drum, to seventy thousand people in Giant Stadium has been incredible to experience. Every step of the way I'm saying to myself, 'Oh my God.' I didn't become a musician to get rich or famous. You aim for the music. The music's the thing. It was a huge relief for me when I just accepted that music is my path and I had faith that music would always provide for me."

"Faith is a good word. Even though my childhood friends at first questioned my relationship with Boyd, I

> " The Dave Matthews Band is definitely a product of musical integration. We all bring a fusion of so many different influences."

always had faith that our love for each other would carry us through. When people meet us as a couple, I never get the sense that anyone questions whether we should be together. We are so obviously a couple. Of course, success and celebrity make people more accepting of a lot of things. We'd run into small, weird tensions when we first started dating that just don't exist anymore. Either that, or I just don't look out for it anymore."

"As a couple, race is not an issue between us, but I definitely run into the subject when I'm out on the road. After being on tour in Europe or Canada, I noticed differences in racial attitudes here in the States. People here seem more suspicious and judgmental. You're so used to this kind of subtle discrimination, that you don't even think about it until you come back from Holland and can feel the difference. In Europe, I'm a musician and here I'm a black musician. We have our own particular brand of issues when it comes to race that don't necessarily translate in other parts of the world. When I hear white members of my health club refer to a forty-five-year-old security guard as a boy, what really saddens me is their total obliviousness to the racism of that observation. It's a feeling of superiority that they don't even realize they have. Just cross the border to Canada and you can experience a country that doesn't have this history of slavery and segregation that we're still trying to recover from. The Dave Matthews Band is definitely a product of musical integration. We all bring a fusion of so many different influences."

"I think our daughter Abby is lucky because she gets to experience the richness of both black and white culture, which is a wonderful kind of cultural fusion that all Americans should share. When she's at Boyd's parents house, everyone is talking at the same time and helping themselves to a lot of food, which is quite different from my family, where words are more cautiously considered and we wait to be offered food. I always thought the, 'What about the children?' line to be a lame excuse to keep the races apart. That was the first thing we heard when we announced our engagement. Boyd had a terrific answer, though. He'd simply say, 'We'll love them.'"

Sitting on the sofa beside her husband of twenty years, Rosalyn says, "My family lived in an experimental, walled-off city block, run by Quakers. Our neighbors were from different economic and racial backgrounds. It was an idyllic place to grow up, but I also knew that directly on the other side of the wall were the projects and gangs. The kids from the projects called me Miss Proper because I didn't speak like them. My parents and grandparents were highly educated and insisted on proper grammar and pronunciation at home."

"Even though we're of different racial backgrounds, our family backgrounds are very similar. We both come from families that are close-knit and put tremendous value on education. My parents' Jewishness made them no strangers to discrimination, so they were as concerned about equal rights as my wife's family."

"One thing that saddens me is that my children are not exposed to more diversity. Most of my kids' classmates at their Montessori school are white, as are our neighbors. The Aryan standard of beauty makes my daughter dislike her hair because it's not blond and straight. She envies her white girlfriends. It breaks my heart to see my beautiful little daughter live in a culture that makes her feel unattractive."

"One advantage that black women have over whites, when it comes to how they feel about their looks, is that most white women never feel 'thin enough,' whereas most black women are a lot more comfortable with their bodies," observes Gordon.

"I remember when I lost a lot of weight so I could fit into my mother's wedding gown. Gordon kept telling me how lovely I looked, but some of my black friends were like, 'What have you done to yourself? You need meat on your bones, woman!' Fragility has had no place in African American history. Both men and women had to be as strong as possible

to survive. I feel very much a part of black culture and history. But Gordon is family, and this is home. I wouldn't want to be told I had to choose between the two. Some of my black friends felt I'd betrayed my race by 'marrying white,' but, over time, they've come to respect our relationship. Still, I'm aware of my race all the time, every day. Too many things happen to ever let you forget that you are judged by the color of your skin. When I was seventeen years old, my white boyfriend instructed me to hide on the floor of his car so his grandmother wouldn't see me. He was afraid if she did, she would disown him from her will. African Americans carry these indignities inside of us. I can happily inhabit an interracial marriage and a predominately white world, but I'm never very far from consciousness of my race..."

> "All African Americans carry these indignities inside of us. I can happily inhabit an interracial marriage and a predominately white world, but I'm never very far away from consciousness of my race..."
> *"...and I hardly ever think of my race, or hers either, for that matter."*

"...and I hardly ever think of my race, or hers either, for that matter," says Gordon.

"When it comes down to it," Rosalyn continues, "there are more similarities than differences among people. We lost our first child to a birth defect and our grief, like our love for each other, was completely the same. The important, human issues transcend race."

Stephanie begins, "I grew up in Chicago, in an all-black, middle class neighborhood. Our family attended a traditional black church. My parents didn't talk about race all that much. But like most black American parents, they taught my sister and me that we'd have to work harder than whites to be successful, and that there were people in the world who would dislike us and try to degrade us solely on the basis of our skin color. They told us these things to prepare us for life. For black children, these lessons are as basic as learning to cross the street. While there was a sense in the community that one should be somewhat cautious in dealing with whites, my parents also taught us to treat everyone with respect and look at people as individuals. Until I moved from my neighborhood school to a magnet school in seventh grade, the only whites I came into regular contact with were a few teachers. The new school drew students from all over the city, so after that I had friends of all races."

"My parents were from rural poverty in Virginia," says Ed, *"and that shaped my life as well as theirs. I think that because my parents' families were poor, other whites often looked down on them or mistreated them. Somehow, I think that made them identify with others who have been mistreated, rather than identify with all whites. Both my parents went on to finish college, and my father earned a graduate degree. Education was a focus in our home. It was a way to prove yourself and open doors. The Durham (NC) schools that I attended as a child were predominately black. It didn't matter to me since my parents never had an issue with it. When I was in junior high, our family really struggled financially, so my brother and I felt some of that same stigma that my parents knew, but to a lesser extent. I know that what we experienced is nothing compared with what blacks have to deal with, but it made me more aware of how I treat others."*

"It wasn't until I went to college at Duke that I had a real struggle with racial issues. A friend from my high school went to a summer orientation program for African American students and came back with all kinds of advice about how to be a black at Duke—don't have too many white friends, join mostly black groups, stick to the black social life—that's what the older Duke students told her. When we got there, I didn't follow these rules, and by the end of the first week, there was a barrier between us. I understood that others wanted and needed a close-knit black community in a mostly white environment, but I resented that they wouldn't accept me unless I accepted their restrictions."

"I noticed some of the same things at Georgetown," Ed adds. "The black students tended to hang out with each other exclusively. I think the students were a reflection of society, with blacks feeling that grievances are

> "I remember when Stephanie was pregnant with Lillian and there was a point when I realized that my child wouldn't have the same privileges of whiteness that I do. I had always been able to choose—again, whether I realized it or not—to confront racial issues, or to avoid them. That's the privilege of whiteness."

not being addressed, and whites feeling like that racism stuff is all over and they've done enough. I could see why the blacks often separate themselves, because most whites don't want to think about racial issues that affect blacks every day of their lives."

"We met through mutual friends at Duke, and were good friends for over a year before we started dating. Once the relationship changed, it got serious pretty quickly. When I first met Ed's parents, it all went well, but I assumed they were just trying to be nice. Afterward I asked Ed what they said when he

told them I was black. 'I didn't tell them,' he said, a little surprised, 'I knew they wouldn't care about that.' My own parents were a little more cautious and afraid that I might get hurt—I think parents of girls always are—but they never discouraged the relationship. They were pretty shocked, though, when we got engaged. What surprised them even more, was how accepting Ed's family was. My dad's from Mississippi, and Ed's parents were not at all like what they expected from southern whites. We've been very blessed that our parents all get along so well. Our mothers even e-mail each other. It's also been great that Lillian can spend time with both sets of grandparents. We've been together for almost ten years, and while racial issues do impact us as a couple, race has never caused a problem between us. I think having support from family is a big part of that."

"My field is southern history and obviously you can't study the history of the South without studying black history. Maybe my southern background has made it possible for me to understand some of these issues a little more quickly than some of my white colleagues. Just as in the last century, in this new century race is still the number one issue that we as a nation have to confront. A large part of the problem is that most whites have a presumption of privilege they don't want to give up. As a white person, it gets on my nerves that so many whites can't see or won't admit they have this sense of entitlement. The attitude that things should go our way, and that non-whites are taking things away from us, as if non-whites don't have as much right to life's privileges as whites do, is a lingering problem in America."

"We're all just deluding ourselves if we deny that we have assumptions about race. Not being honest about it just holds us back. For example, if I'm not treated well by a white salesperson, I might assume that the salesperson doesn't value me as a customer because I'm black. That might not always be true, but that's where my mind goes. I think just about everyone who grows up in America has that sort of negative attitude embedded in our thinking, and we need to call ourselves on it."

"When I'm out alone, people just see a white guy. For the most part, I benefit from that whether I intend to or not. We're expecting a second child now. I remember when Stephanie was pregnant with Lillian and there was a point when I realized that my child wouldn't have the same privileges of whiteness that I do. I had always been able to choose – again, whether I realized it or not—to confront racial issues, or to avoid them. That's the privilege of whiteness. Now, in a way, I've lost some of that privilege to choose. As Lillian grows up, she'll have to deal with all of the problems that go along with being black, as well as the assumptions that both races put on biracial people. We'll have to teach her that you can't stop other people from putting labels on you, but you don't have to accept those labels.

grew up as a Catholic in a predominately white town in New Jersey," begins Crystal, as she serves supper while rocking the baby's swing. "I was one of two black kids in the entire school system, [K through 12]. In third grade the only other black kid left and it was just me for a long time. I was never allowed not to think about it for too long, because everyone always reminded me in one way or another. My mom thought it was very important that I be exposed to the African American community, so she'd send me to stay with relatives in D.C. during the summer."

"The funny part was, she'd come back from summer vacation speaking like the inner city black kids, and her mom didn't like that too much either," laughs David, as he carries lemonade to the table while hopping on one leg. (He lost the other in Vietnam.)

"Now my dad was from Africa, so he had no clue about African American culture before living here," continues Crystal. "I was able to visit relatives in Liberia, so I was able to absorb and appreciate that part of my heritage as well. Now I'm very grateful for my background, but as a kid, it was very tough to feel comfortable with my identity. Especially in high school, it's hard when you don't look like everyone else and are raised by culturally diverse parents."

"Her father came here in the 1960s and was completely unfamiliar with social customs concerning race."

"That's right! Remember that story he used to tell about him knocking on some white family's door and asking to use the phone, and they're scared out of their wits, but he doesn't know why?"

"I grew up in a restricted town, though I didn't realize it growing up. I remember seeing a black kid walking through our street and wondering why he looked completely terrified. Of course, I was too naive to know that it probably wasn't a safe neighborhood for him to venture through. One of the neighborhood kids said, 'Look at that nigger.' Now, I had never heard that word before and hardly ever seen any black people. So a week later, when my dad is driving me through a section of Newark, I blurt out,

through the open windows of our car, 'Wow, look at all those niggers walking around!' My father turns to me and says firmly and slowly, 'David, that's not a very nice word. That's not a word that we use.'"

"I was a third-year medical student when we met. David was teaching swimming at the children's rehab center, but we'd already met several times through mutual friends."

"Even though I had never dated anyone of another race before, we had so many common interests that it seemed completely natural that we'd spend time together."

"We both love all kinds of music, especially classical music, and outdoor activities, especially water sports. Because of David's previous history with medical institutions, he's always had a very good

> "Most white upper middle class southerners had blacks preparing their food, raising their children, and caring for their valuables, yet they wouldn't sit next to them in a restaurant or movie theater."

understanding of my work."

"I was injured by a mine in Vietnam in 1970 and spent a year and a half in the hospital. I got to know a lot of doctors and started doing medical photography while I was still a patient."

"We became serious about each other fairly quickly, and even though my parents had always taught us to treat everyone equally, they were less than thrilled with my relationship with David ."

"That's an understatement," adds David, with no resentment, but warmth and humor. "They hated the idea!"

"You'd think my mom would have been more sympathetic, because her family didn't approve of her marrying an African. My mother wouldn't even tell my dad about us. She made me tell him how serious we were about staying together. Once that became apparent, I was really afraid that I'd lose my relationship with my parents and my sister. It was a very tough time for me. I ended up seeing a shrink."

"The disapproval wasn't just about my race, but the fact that Crystal made a decision without his approval, that really tore the family apart for a while. He didn't know what he wanted for her, but he knew what he didn't want—a one legged, underemployed, much older white man!"

"He wouldn't have wanted me to marry a Liberian or an African American either. It's hard to imagine who he'd pick out for me to marry. And my mom's thing was that marriage was hard enough without having to deal with the race issue. But our feeling was if we could weather the crisis of our engagement, we could overcome just about anything down the road."

"That kind of pressure to break up makes you ask, 'Is this really worth

> "I felt a lot of disapproval from my black friends when David and I got engaged. They interpreted my feeling for David as a rejection of black men, which is untrue and unfair."

it?' More so for Crystal then for me, because my grief was seeing what she was going through. My family really loved Crystal and gave us their blessing from the beginning."

Crystal's voice fills with emotion as she recalls, "My mother wanted to go to the wedding, but my father said he wouldn't go. When she told me that she couldn't come without him, it was a pivotal moment for both of us. The moment when I really became my own person was when I said, 'You promised me you would always be there for me and so I'm very disappointed.' The next day she told me she'd come, even if he wouldn't. They'd always done important family events together and this was the first time she'd potentially go it alone."

"He did eventually show up for the ceremony and reception. He didn't want to look like the bad guy. He even stood up and gave a toast. It was more than a little strained and stayed that way until the grandchildren arrived. He couldn't be a better grandfather. I know we'll never be best buddies, but just seeing the way he truly loves our kids really goes a long way to make the memories of the way he rejected me fade."

"Just like I was surprised that it was my own family that disapproved of us more than strangers, we've been pleasantly surprised that living in South Carolina hasn't been as difficult for us as we feared. Maybe it's because the Deep South has always had blacks and whites living side by side. When we're in the mall with our daughters, people stop us all the time and tell us how beautiful our kids are. I'm amazed that our family is not only tolerated, but really appreciated."

"But Charleston is not like most of the state," says David. "The state constitution prohibited interracial marriage until recently. They had a public referendum, and thirty-eight percent of the population voted to keep the laws on the books, even though the supreme court struck down the legality of those laws over thirty years ago."

"Seeing a black woman with a white man is so rare. I felt a lot of disapproval from my black friends when David and I got engaged. They interpreted my feeling for David as a rejection of black men, which is untrue and unfair."

"What really makes us laugh, is when we see a white woman with black kids. So often, the little girl's hair is a fright because her mom doesn't know how to take care of it. One of the first things I learned about Crystal's hair is that she doesn't want to get it wet! I know how much time she has to spend on her hair to keep it the way she likes it to look."

"I can't tell you how many times I've wanted to take a white mother aside and show her what to do with black hair."

"When you see a biracial kid, you can almost always tell whether the mother is black or white by the way their hair is fixed..."

"...or not fixed!" laughs Crystal.

"It's interesting that yesterday our daughter Ciaran was drawing a picture of Crystal, and she made her have really curly hair, even though she doesn't wear it that way. She's very matter of fact about the differences in

our coloring. She says, 'Mommy's dark brown and Daddy's light brown.'

"The sad truth, though, is there comes a day for every woman of color, when they realize that their looks do not conform with society's standards of beauty. I went through it. My sister, who's twelve years younger, went through it. And I'm afraid that my two girls will too. It saddens me to think that no matter how much we tell them that everyone's equal, there'll come a time when the rules don't apply and some people will seem more privileged than others through no efforts of their own. I remember telling my dad, when I was six or seven, that I want to be white. Of course, my parents were terribly upset, but my mother understood. What I really meant was that I wanted to be accepted and appreciated for who I am. That I didn't want to be looked at as different."

"What we as a society have to come to accept is that we're all mixed and we're all different. My family roots have all different nationalities. Crystals' mother has both Indian and white blood, even though she considers herself an African American. Even though everyone has their differences, they also have their similarities. One of my first impressions of Crystal was that she had Vivaldi playing in her car. She told me about her love for baroque music and I was impressed by our common ground."

"Even though both my parents are black, David and I have a lot more in common because we're both Americans. My mom converted to my dad's Catholicism, but since I was raised in the Irish-Polish Catholic Church, I was right at home with David's Irish Catholic background. For us, there's a lot more difference between the Liberian culture and African American culture than there is between the white American culture and the black American culture. I don't think our marriage has to surmount as many obstacles as my career has. When people see me in the hospital with my white coat and stethoscope, they automatically think I'm a nurse, or a lower rank in the hierarchy of medicine. The medical system is still very much a good old boy network, even with larger numbers of blacks and women going to medical school. It takes generations for things to change more than superficially. The interesting thing is my most outwardly appreciative patients are usually older white men. They just love me. Maybe they had black nurse maids growing up and feel really safe in my presence. The older men want to hug me every chance they get!"

"It's something we've talked about before," says David. "Many of the older white adults in South Carolina were raised by black women. It's weird when you think about the fact that most white upper middle class southerners had blacks preparing their food, raising their children, and caring for their valuables, yet they wouldn't sit next to them in a restaurant or movie theater. The dichotomy of that system is amazing to think about. How can you give people you distrust and disrespect the responsibility of caring for everything that matters to you? The confusion of such hypocrisy goes farther back than Thomas Jefferson and forward beyond Clarence Thomas."

When we were dating, we ordered some ice cream. When Jim's arrived first, I started to eat a few bites and the waitress took the spoon out of my hand and gave him another spoon."

"She just assumed I wouldn't want to share the same utensil," adds Jim.

"And I started eating with that one too."

"And darned if she didn't grab that one from Gloria also!"

"Jim had to speak up and say, 'Look, we're dating—we're living together—we can share a spoon!' We weren't about to let her ignorance keep us from doing what we set out to do—which was enjoy our ice cream!"

"I grew up in Lynchburg, Virginia, and I'm old enough to remember when our state was very segregated, so I can't say I'm totally surprised when people make racist assumptions. In fact, I probably just assumed that I'd only date white women, until I met Gloria."

"We had so many of the same interests. I think he was surprised that I liked to go camping, because it's hardly a black pastime. We both like to play tennis and shoot pool, so we were always doing things together."

"I'd never met anyone who I had so much to talk about with, but I was amazed to find myself falling in love. Frankly, I was scared to death, because I knew the cost would be tremendous. When we got married, the only co-workers who came to the wedding were my black friends. My parents certainly didn't show up! Around the office, people were saying it would never last, but I think after twenty some years we're accepted as the real thing."

"My family was supportive from the beginning, but it took grandchildren to build a bridge back to Jim's parents. My mother taught me that you don't fight fire with fire, you fight fire with sugar. I always spoke nicely about his folks to our three kids. I would always show them photos of Jim's parents and when I finally introduced our daughter to Jim's dad as Mr. Fox, she pipes up with, 'That's not Mr. Fox, that's Grandpa!' Well that was it—the walls came tumbling down."

"After that, they'd call on the phone and ask Gloria what the twins

would like for Christmas. That's a long way from when they used to call me and not even acknowledge that my wife or children existed."

"I think it's blown my in-laws' minds and opened their hearts to watch our beautiful girls grow and develop a lot of the same characteristics that Jim and his sisters have. I could show you baby pictures of Jim's family that look just like our twins. It seems like kids can get a whole lot of good stuff started."

"Our kids got us going to church, which is probably one of the most important things in our lives."

"That's right!" says Gloria, obviously delighted. "They came home from school and asked if they could go to church like their schoolmates."

"Even though I'm the only white person at our church, I feel right at home. I even brought my dad here and he was moved by the preaching

> "I'd never met anyone who I had so much to talk about with, but I was amazed to find myself falling in love. Frankly, I was scared to death, because I knew the cost would be tremendous. When we got married, the only co-workers who came to the wedding were my black friends. My parents certainly didn't show up!"

and the music."

"We're a completely integrated couple." Gloria reaches over and takes Jim's hand before continuing. "We live in a racially mixed neighborhood, while our church is almost all black. One of our twin daughters dates a white guy and has mostly white friends, whereas the other one has a black boyfriend and mostly black friends."

1 grew up on a dairy farm in England," begins Sally, with her British accent. "There were no other houses for miles around. Dad built the house in the middle of a cornfield and I used to play there with my cousins."

"Growing up in Watts, California," laughs Bozz, "my childhood was a long way from a cornfield. I watched the gang fights go from fist fights to knifings to shootings as drugs came into the neighborhood. The riots of '65 made us sleep under our beds. As soon as I graduated from high school I left there and went to live in Utah with the Mormons. Job Corps was my ticket out of there."

"Bozz and I had a very short courtship. We were working at the same school on the Mojave desert. On our first date he picked me up at 3:00 and by 9:00 we were engaged! We immediately realized that we had the same goals in life even though we came from totally separate backgrounds. Three weeks later we were married."

"I was immediately attracted to Sally's rural innocence. I knew that had more value to me than street smarts. My family tree is a complete melting pot, so Sally's race and nationality was never any obstacle for me at all. I did the Pan African thing—I was black to the bone, but I came to realize that I'm a spiritual being, a citizen of the planet earth. A lot of the people I grew up with are no longer on this planet. The things my friends got into precipitated their early demise. Early on I realized that I couldn't fight my way out of poverty, that I'd have to produce my way out. Through Job Corps I learned to work with plastics and I started working for Disney, making plastic animals for their different theme park exhibits. Now I work with Mission Renaissance Fine Arts Classes. I feel completely lucky to be working in such a creative environment. I feel grateful that my daughter won't have to deal with the things I had to grow up with. She won't have that segregated consciousness of Watts, where it's 'the white man is this' or 'the black man is that.' It's not really productive to keep focusing on all the injustices blacks suffered at the hands of whites. The only way to move forward is to look forward and not let the past make you feel like a victim. Forty acres and a mule won't do me much good today anyway. Speaking correctly is much more

important. If your English is not up to par, you're really holding yourself back. In a funny way, I'm an immigrant like Sally: I taught myself good grammar and moved out of the inner city. I go back to the old neighborhood now and help kids improve their communication skills. I believe very strongly that we have to be responsible not only for ourselves, but also for those who want our help."

"From the beginning I realized that Bozz was very spiritual and young-at-heart. I loved his enthusiasm and honesty. He made me feel safe to be myself."

"Being a musician, I was aware from early on that each individual is a spiritual being and that's where the music comes from."

"You can take more control of your environment than most people realize," says Sally. "We've decided not to have TV in the house, and we're going to homeschool Camilla. You have more choices than you sometimes

> "Forty acres and a mule won't do me much good today. Speaking correctly is much more important. If your English is not up to par, you're really holding yourself back."

appreciate. Public education isn't interested in teaching kids how to think, and we want our daughter to think for herself. She's got dual citizenship as well as being biracial. We want her to get her identity from her own sense of uniqueness instead of from any group."

"If folks could hold on to the idea that we're all individuals, instead of 'you people' or 'those people,' there would be less suspicion and more respect. Society and history is made up of many individual stories. That's why that United Colors of Bennetton ad campaign is so powerful, because the portraits of all the different races shows the equal worth of each individual. I say keep putting it out there—that people are different but the same."

My dad worked for a chemical company and we moved around a lot, including Europe my senior year in high school," says Liz.

"I was born and raised in Cleveland, never going much of anywhere until I went to college. The public school system in Cleveland isn't too great, so I went to Catholic schools, even though my family isn't Catholic. My mom's a teacher and she's getting her master's degree at the same time I'm getting my diploma this May. My parents have three kids in college and one still in high school. Obviously education is not optional in my family. We had to wear uniforms in my Jesuit high school and would stick out like sore thumbs on the East Side, walking home from school. Running home is more like it, because we got out five minutes before Audubon [the local public school] and I wanted to make it home before the kids could tease me. It was good practice for track, running to and from Saint Ignatius every day," laughs Raymond, who is now on his university track and cross country team.

"Raymond and I met when we were both working at a summer camp. We were good friends for a long time before we started dating. We'd play a lot of sports together and just hang out. Over time I realized that I like spending time with him more than anyone else."

"I found Liz unique from the beginning. The first day we met I went to go play basketball with some of the other counselors and I didn't realize that there was a girl playing with us. It was Liz! I'd never known anyone like her. She'd take me to Skyline Drive just to watch the leaves change. That is not something I would regularly choose to do! Liz always has a plan. She'll have me making pottery or playing field hockey, things I'd never think of doing on my own."

"My parents raised me to seek out experience more than stuff. I'll bargain hunt for clothes and only buy things I really need, yet will spend big bucks in a good restaurant or for a theater ticket. I think a nice thing that's come out of my relationship with Raymond is that it forced my parents to test their ideology. Your ideology is not concrete until it's tested. They taught me to judge things by their true worth, so Raymond's race did not play a factor in my feelings towards him, it just felt right."

"I'd never dated outside of my race before, and I think I was a little bit shocked to find myself falling for Liz. My family faced that test too, of facing their deepest true feelings about race, and came out on the other side accepting us as a couple."

"I think most parents carry this image of who they imagine their child will choose as a partner, and if that person doesn't look like that image, it can take a while to come to terms with that contradiction. Images of mixed couples in this society are still unusual. When I see another interracial couple, I tend to stare, because I find it reaffirming. Of course, they might not know that!"

"Both of us are interested in the subject of race as far as it pertains to U.S. History, but we don't sit around and talk about how it affects us as a

> "One thing that's hard for most white people to understand is this race responsibility that African Americans carry around with them. As both a student and an athlete I feel like my entire race is being judged by my individual behavior."

couple, because I don't think it does," says Raymond.

"We had one moment," continues Liz, "when I asked, 'Does this matter?' It was one question. Answer. Done. To me, our differences just make the relationship more interesting and fulfilling, because we have so much to learn from each other."

"I break quite a few stereotypes. I'm majoring in education, and I'm one of the few black milers on the track team. Most African Americans are sprinters. I've even had coaches say to me, 'I didn't know black people ran

cross country.' I surprised a lot of people when I was voted MVP last season. I do have this sense of responsibility to teach kids in the inner city when I graduate. I grew up in those neighborhoods and I'd like to go back and make a difference. I want to live there as well as work there, because it's not enough just to drive in, do your lessons, then turn around and leave after class. One thing that's hard for most white people to understand is this race responsibility that African Americans carry around with them. As both a student and an athlete I feel like my entire race is being judged by my individual behavior."

"Raymond and I have recently talked a lot about language and the differences in speech patterns

"A nice thing that's come out of my relationship with Raymond is that it forced my parents to test their ideology. They taught me to judge things by their true worth, so Raymond's race did not play a factor in my feelings towards him."

between African Americans and Anglo Americans. It's interesting to realize that he's so aware of what speech he uses in front of different audiences."

"There are definitely phrases that I would use at home or in my neighborhood that I wouldn't be comfortable using in the classroom. Black English has a different structure and rhythm. Of course, almost all Americans speak their own brand of English, depending on where and how they were raised."

"One thing that Raymond and I have in common is that we both tend to push ourselves into situations where we might be in the minority, whether it's me playing basketball with the boys or Raymond running cross country. As a child, I felt this tremendous sense of unfairness about how girls were treated differently and I think Raymond's parochial school education certainly put him outside of the comfort zone of society's expectations. Both of us want to make a difference by working with at-risk kids. Both of us want to avoid complacency. For some reason, if you're a minority, you're defined by your race more than any other characteristics."

"A lot of times you're told that that's what you are. You're the black whatever, fill in the blank. The black education student, the black cross country runner. It seems like your race precedes any other definition."

"I find it interesting that while Raymond and I have been working to maintain our relationship since I graduated and work in another town, people who don't know us well will just assume that race is an obstacle in our relationship. Since society tends to judge us by our external appearance, the true breadth of our relationship is glanced over. Any kind of partnership is challenging and I find it sad that society sees race as the challenge, instead of recognizing the beauty and difficulty of maintaining any healthy relationship."

Doug recalls the optimism of his younger days. "The early seventies were a very different time than now. Even though both of our parents voiced initial opposition to our marriage because of our different races, the times were filled with the possibility of a truly integrated society."

"Back then, it was just taken for granted that biracial children would have a lot of emotional problems," continues Suzanne, *"and my dad was worried for us about that. This stereotype had no real basis in fact, and I never believed it for a second. The birth of our first child laid his fears to rest. It marked the end of any hesitation that my dad had about our union. Our son was the most beautiful baby any of us had ever laid eyes on."*

"In some ways African Americans are more balkanized today than they were twenty-five years ago. Look at any high school cafeteria today. You'd think the segregation laws were back on the books. In my mind, there's only one legitimate minority, and that's the individual. Once any group demands entitlement, there's resentment all around. If you apply a remedy to a symptom instead of to the problem itself, the remedy will eventually become a problem, whether it's welfare or affirmative action."

Their fifteen-year-old daughter, Ahvery, joins in the conversation and says, "I've never felt any mistreatment because I'm biracial. My grandfather shouldn't have had a moment's worry about the plight of his grandchildren because I'm doing very well indeed."

"Just look at her," beams her proud father. "She shows what can happen when we work together. A beautiful result."

"My brother, sister, and

I have been lucky to go to private school. There just aren't the same kind of cliques, where you have to choose a peer group. All the kids at my school just accept each other as fellow students. We all have the common goal of valuing a good education. It's not about separating into different racial or ethnic groups."

"Nowadays it seems like many people never talk about how things should be, they just complain about how things are. If you close your eyes and point at anything around you, that object at one time was a dream in someone's mind before it became a reality. If we're ever going to have a reality that we can live with, we are going to have to dream it first, and then make that dream a reality. It's a lot easier to be negative than to struggle to make a change."

> "In some ways African Americans are more balkanized today than they were twenty-five years ago. Look at any high school cafeteria today. You'd think the segregation laws were back on the books."

Susanne sighs, "The assassination of Martin Luther King was more terrible than we could ever have realized at the time, because this country lost a great visionary who was working towards the very positive dream of equality and justice. As a nation, over the last two decades, we've lost our ability to dream."

"There's a whole generation of people who have given up dreaming, in order to be right. We believe in the innate potential of every human being to evolve and become better. Our children are part of that dream."

"Chester and I lived next door to each other as kids," begins Michelle, "though I spent more time playing with his younger brother back then because he was more my age."

"We re-met twenty years later, after we'd both been married and divorced," says Chester. *"It was the strangest thing because, even though we didn't recognize each other after all those years, we didn't want to let go of each other's hands when we were introduced. I called her on the phone later that night and asked her to meet me at her old address, and when she said she used to live in that house when she was a little girl, I knew she was the girl next door."*

"Two weeks later, we were married! I know it sounds strange, but I knew we'd be mates the moment we shook hands. It felt very much like coming home. Being with Chester is like rediscovering the happiness of my childhood."

"I'd never dated a white woman before Michelle. I guess I was just waiting for the right one to come along. I never had a moment's doubt that Michelle and I weren't meant to be together. Our first real discussion was about our attitudes towards race."

"He just came right out and asked me, 'How do you feel about black people?' I just laughed out loud at the question, saying people are people, no matter their race, and some are great and some are not so great. On our second date we were talking about what our goals were for a marriage. We agreed on everything. He kept saying, 'I would marry you in a minute.' So I said, 'Let's go!'"

Chester continues, "When we went to the magistrate's office to get our marriage license, the clerk behind the desk said, 'You don't need to tell me why you're here, it's obvious you want to get married!'"

"Until we met, or re-met, I suppose, I'd never had such a strong sense of belonging as I did with him. His mother brought out a family photo album and showed us a picture of me when I was a nine years old."

"In my lifetime I've seen race relations between black and white come a long way towards healing. There was a time when I almost hated white folks because of the way they used to treat us. When John Kennedy was

> "In my lifetime I've seen race relations between black and white come a long way towards healing. There was a time when I almost hated white folks because of the way they used to treat us. Now the love of my life is a white person."

assassinated, I realized that not all white people wanted to keep blacks down. Once I let go of that hatred, I started to feel better about myself. Now the love of my life is a white person. Once the family is integrated, the barriers between the races are down."

"I believe that deep inside, people know the difference between right and wrong," says Michelle. "Racism is just wrong. It's wrong to hate someone that you don't even know. The concept of slavery and segregation is evil and that's why it didn't last."

grew up in extremely modest circumstances in Portsmouth, Virginia," says Milton. "It was a big deal when we got an indoor bathroom. When I was about eleven or twelve, our home was bought out by developers and we were suddenly middle class suburbanites. My school went from being one hundred percent black and poor to mostly white and middle class. We were sort of like the Beverly Hillbillies—it was such a drastic transition!"

"We certainly came from different backgrounds," says Regina. "I was raised in a Mennonite community in Pennsylvania. Just being raised without a television set in the house helped make me different from my peers. One thing that made me immediately feel close to Milton was that he could relate to the lifestyle differences that my Christianity asks of me because his mother's Pentecostal church also demanded certain behaviors that weren't always mainstream."

"We met in 1977, at MCV emergency room, where she was a nurse and I was an X-ray technologist. At that time everyone was wearing miniskirts, except Regina, who wore these calf length dresses and I thought she was very interesting."

"As far as our different races were concerned, there was no boundary for me to think about. I was not exposed to overt prejudice growing up. The church taught me that we're all God's children, and there's no Biblical scripture that prohibits interracial marriage."

"I'd always been one to be away from the herd, so I don't think my family was particularly surprised when we fell in love. They were much more baffled when I started dancing with the Richmond ballet than when I showed up with Regina! I remember when I was a football player in high school and the black female students there wanted us to boycott the team because there were no black cheerleaders at the time. My feeling was everyone is on their own to earn what they get

and no one is entitled. I'd worked hard for my position on the team and I felt the girls would have to do the same. Because I'm African American, I feel like people make assumptions about my politics. My neighbors call me a closet Republican, but the truth of the matter is I don't feel much allegiance towards either party. In Richmond, VA, politics tends to fall along racial lines, but the color of my skin doesn't control my thoughts on every issue. Blind allegiance to race instead of policy just increases the divide between black and white in this country. Black Americans almost have to choose between maintaining their cultural identity or moving on to a more homogenous mainstream, and that's a very painful crossroads that you have to cross more than once if you continue to achieve."

> "Black Americans almost have to choose between maintaining their cultural identity or moving on to a more homogenous mainstream, and that's a very painful crossroads that you have to cross more than once if you continue to achieve."

"It seems to me," Regina interjects, "that it's easy to confuse culture with race. The music, food, dress, and language of black Americans is cultural, not racial."

"Your race is a constant, but cultural attitudes shift. As a child, I identified myself as a Negro. By my late teens, I was Black and now I'm supposed to be identified as African American. I might get a new identifying label every ten years, but my race stays the same, no matter what you call it."

"One reason we homeschool our children is we want their identity to

come from their own self-awareness and not be placed on them by the school system or their peers. We don't want them to be categorized and possibly limited academically by some teacher's static expectations. We seem to have our own timeline for life. We're both late bloomers. We dated for six years before we got married and were married seven years before we had kids, so you can see, we are not rushed by other people's expectations."

"I think there's too much pressure on children too soon in schools today," says Milton. "We both feel that at this point in their lives that they're better off being taught by their parents."

"Music has always been an important part of my life and that's an important part of their education," continues Regina. "We can guide our children in our own values more easily when we don't hand them over to the public school system. There you deal with families that function totally inside popular culture, and we're just not comfortable raising our children with those values. We frequently ask ourselves, 'What part of popular culture can we be involved in, or when does following Christ call us apart?' In regard to our children, their spiritual identity is more important to us than the race issue."

"In the last twenty years we've very rarely had to put up with much disapproval or hostility because of our different races. We sort of inadvertently stumbled on to one of the most integrated neighborhoods in town."

"If anything, it seems like people make a point of saying how

beautiful our children are. "It feels like an intentional affirmation. Before I had kids, I wondered if it would be a problem for me if they were a different color than me, but love knows no color. Your child is simply your child and there's nothing there to feel odd about. Your feel as devoted and

> "Before I had kids, I wondered if it would be a problem for me if they were a different color than me, but love knows no color. Your child is simply your child and there's nothing there to feel odd about."

protective as a lioness. One thing that's kind of interesting is I feel like I'm more accepted by black folks when they see me with my children, because they can tell right away that I'm not racist! As far as being a biracial family is concerned, it's not a major issue in our life."

"As far as our nation's attitudes towards race is concerned," says Milton, "we're still in the process of waiting for the generations to turn over. Attitudes can and do change, but not completely in one lifetime."

"It's hard for me to believe that it was illegal for Milton and I to be married in Virginia until the late sixties! We've come a long way as an integrated society, but we've still got a long way to go."

I joined up with the Air Force after high school and served in Vietnam. After being stationed in Bermuda, Florida, and Hawaii, I couldn't go back to the cold dark winters of the Northeast. After I got out of the service, I moved back to Hawaii, which is where I met Martha."

"I transferred from George Washington University in D.C. to the University of Hawaii," says Martha, "because I was restless to see more of the world. I liked it so much that I stayed and started working for the Church of Scientology in 1980."

"I worked for the Hawaii church for five years. I was first introduced to Scientology when I was stationed in Hawaii. When I read L. Ron Hubbard's *Dianetics, The Modern Science of Mental Health*, it just made a lot of sense."

"It's so important to both of us and that's a big bond between us. There's so much interracial mixing in Hawaii, that our different races never seemed like much of a problem."

"One thing most Americans forget is that, globally, whites are a tiny proportion of the population. As a black American, who was always referred to as a minority at home, it was a revelation to me to see all the brown skin peoples in the Philippines, Bermuda, Jamaica, and even Hawaii."

"We left Hawaii and moved to southern California for our kids' education. Mixed marriages here are completely common. We've never felt uncomfortable or apologetic about being a mixed race couple. Of course, within the Church of Scientology, one's race is not important."

"What you read in the paper or see on TV isn't always a realistic portrayal of what it's like to actually be in that place. The media makes earthquakes seem like a Hollywood disaster film. More people die shoveling snow than in earthquakes, but you never hear about that. The Rodney King riots were played up like a racial apocalypse. Our integrated life never makes the news because things are fine. One of the tenets of Scientology is that people are basically good. You can only oppress people for so long before they rise up and say, 'Enough, this isn't fair.' Slavery and communism didn't last because they deny basic human integrity."

"What attracted me to Scientology in the first place," says Martha, "is the belief in the human potential to evolve towards goodness. Each individual can make the world a better place by improving their own behavior. There's no such thing as 'those people.' Each person is their own unique individual."

"Racism is a contagion of insanity. One generation passes it on to the next. Martha and I have made a family that stops the insanity. Our kids don't have anything invested in identifying with being black or white."

"One reason we have our kids in private school is that we feel like the public schools are totally obsessed with race and culture. If you keep

> "Each individual can make the world a better place by improving their own behavior. There's no such thing as 'those people.' Each person is their own unique individual."

focusing on that stuff, it does much more harm than good. In our children's school, race and ethnicity are not the be-all end-all."

"Man is a spiritual being, and the body is just a shell, not the essence of the man," says Larry. "Once you realize this, race and culture seem insignificant. Back when I was in the service in the early seventies, race relations was a huge subject and we had to go to all these classes. I remember thinking that all their good intentions just made things worse for everyone. We've become such a nation of whiners and victims. Everyone would be better off if we'd take responsibility for our own behavior and spend less time holding others responsible."

We've been together for over twenty-three years now," says Madeline. "Chris was a lifeguard at my sister's apartment complex in Maryland when we first met."

"I come from a large Irish Catholic family in Pittsburgh. My father was bigoted against blacks and most other ethnic groups. Somehow none of us were affected by his prejudices. When we were kids, our favorite sports heroes were the black players. Roberto Clemente was both black and Hispanic, which drove my father nuts. We grew up listening to Motown music and admiring Martin Luther King, Jr. By the time Madeline and I became a couple, I was totally estranged from him, so they never met. Why expose her to his bigotry?"

"I've never carried my blackness as my primary identity. It might be one of the first characteristics that someone else notices about me, but it's not the first thing I identify with when I describe my humanity. I'm not in denial about my race, but I'm not obsessed either. The media tends to play the race card with every news story it can. It fans the flames of guilt and suspicion across the color line."

"The Rodney King riots and the O.J. Simpson trial revealed to White America the bad blood between the police and black Americans. On the other hand, it also seems like blacks are frequently hypersensitive, seeing every slight and setback as racism. This can cloud the real issue. I remember when a black woman on the street was begging for money and when I walked by her she yelled at me, 'I bet if I was white, you'd give me some money!' I stopped and showed her a picture of my wife and kids. Both blacks and whites have to stop jumping to conclusions about each other. It's a lot easier to react to the prejudice of others than it is to confront your own prejudices."

Ten-year-old Daniel joins in and says, "When I tell kids I'm a mix of black and white, they sometimes call me an Oreo, which is ridiculous because, do I look like a cookie to you? All this name calling about color is silly because color is only skin deep. It's only a thin layer of who you are.

I'm not black. I'm not white. I'm tan."

"I've coined the word 'Afro-Irish American' for our kids," laughs Chris. "You've got to keep a sense of humor, or we'd all go crazy. Sometimes good intentions can be painfully misguided. Dan's teacher did this exercise where she separated the white kids from the non-white kids. The white kids were allowed to go outside to play and the non-white kids had to stay inside and clean the classroom. Then the two groups were supposed to switch places. However, when the white kids got back into the classroom, the room had already been cleaned up, so it was just more fun playtime for them. What the teacher didn't know was that Daniel looked in the window and saw the white kids playing. Well, he was so mad about this that he ended up hitting one of the white kids. When I heard about this, I asked

> "When I tell kids I'm a mix of black and white, they sometimes call me an Oreo, which is ridiculous because, do I look like a cookie to you?"

Daniel if he was mad at the boy he hit and he said, 'No—I was mad at the teacher, but I couldn't hit her!'"

Daniel explains, "It seemed like all the white kids were being treated like royalty that day and all the non-white kids, even though they were good that day, were treated the opposite. It made me feel angry because it was so unfair. The non-white kids did all the clean-up work and the white kids had all the fun!"

"I have this theory about the TV show Star Trek, and why it was so popular," concludes Chris. "It portrayed a future wherein all the races were fully integrated and women were treated equally. It was a vision of how the human race could be."

We both were born and raised in Louisville, Kentucky and we met on my twenty-first birthday through mutual friends."

"*I made sure to get her phone number and knew right away that I definitely wanted to see her again. Her race didn't matter to me one way or another—I liked her smile and thought she was really nice," says Greg.*

"Both of us had dated outside of our race before, and it wasn't an issue when we first started going out. My first grade teacher was a black woman who was a screamer, and it made me not only terrified of going to school, but fearful of all black people. My parents worked really hard to teach me not to be afraid. In fact, today they tease me that they really did a good job! Not only did I overcome my budding racism, but I'm now a first grade teacher myself—and I used to have a real school phobia."

"*She certainly conquered her childhood fears," laughs Greg. "My family lived in a predominately white neighborhood and I went to private school in the early grades, so I was always comfortable around both races.*"

"I think it's more difficult for a white person to have an understanding of black culture, because society as a whole is based on white culture. I sometimes wonder what it would be like to live in a society where most of the movies, TV shows, advertising and people in charge were black. I think living with Greg has made me more sensitive to the importance of exposing my students to stories of all different races and cultures. Children need inspirational role models that are their same sex and race. My family was pretty typical in their attitude towards race relations. They were very concerned that I overcome my fear of blacks, but they did not approve when I started dating a black guy in high school. It was OK to be friends, but anything closer was stepping over an invisible line. I kept my relationship with Greg secret from them until we decided to get engaged. They were tremendously supportive of Greg once they met him."

"*Both of our families have been great. We've been really blessed in the love and support they've given us," adds Greg.*

"We'd love to have children. I've had two miscarriages, but we believe one day we'll have a family."

"*In the five years that we've been married, we've really noticed an increase in interracial couples. I think the children of those marriages are important in the healing process between blacks and whites.*"

"The ironic thing about mixed marriage is that everyone's concerned about the children of those unions—that's the 'big fear.' Yet when the 'big fear' arrives, it's very often the thing that makes both sides of the family closer. Even though I'm too young to remember legalized segregation, as a mixed couple we certainly get some stares and sometimes you can't help but wonder if bad service at a restaurant isn't some weird form of disapproval. And then you wonder if you're being paranoid. These are issues white people never have to wrestle with unless their mate is black.

"Look at our pit bulls. These are the sweetest pets, but a lot of people automatically think they're vicious killers because of the sensational publicity surrounding the breed. As a black male, I realize how damaging bad publicity can be for any group."

There's certainly a lot of people out there in the world who are against us. There are neighborhoods in Louisville where we would not be welcome. We'd probably not even be safe. But these aren't things we dwell on. We'd rather count our blessings."

"*Our faith in the Lord is the bedrock of our relationship. Wars have been fought over the differences in religions, just like the differences in cultures or races, but I believe that religions and people have more in* common than they do differences. A lot of times we get lost in this quagmire of subtle differences, and never emerge from it. I went to Moorehouse College in Atlanta. It's all black and all male, and I found it to be a very sterile environment because it didn't mirror the world that we live in. I did come to appreciate, however, a lot of things about my heritage that I might not have realized if I hadn't been immersed in black culture. I also came to realize that people are people and a black knucklehead is as bad as a white knucklehead!"

"So many things that we perceive as rude or irritating are really just cultural differences," says Jennifer.

"Like when we go to the movies and she's shushing me because I'm talking through the previews!"

"Or when we visit Greg's family during the holidays. The difference between being with our two families is huge. At his parents', there's music on while everyone's talking at the same time. At my house, there's no music and people speak quietly, one at a time. I actually treasure the opportunity to enjoy two different cultures. Getting to know his family has taught me a lot about my own."

"I wish people could just open themselves up to the rightness of many different ways to do the same thing. There are many ways to be a family, a church, a school or a community. Just because you choose one way, doesn't mean everyone else is wrong. I believe that people who feel threatened by other cultures or races are those who don't have a strong sense of identity themselves. Anyone else's differentness is scary to them..."

> "The ironic thing about mixed marriage is that everyone's concerned about the children of those unions—that's the 'big fear.' Yet when the 'big fear' arrives, it's very often the thing that makes both sides of the family closer.

"...and that's a shame," adds Jennifer, "because you cheat yourself out of the ability to look at things from different perspectives. If you're not open to things, you miss a lot."

"I look at each person that I meet as a mirror that casts back a little glimpse of myself. If you have a negative attitude, you're going to get negative reflections back. Preconceived notions just make us blind to what really is. No one is totally free from inherent biases, but we have to be aware of how our past experiences affect our present reactions if we're really going to experience things openly and honestly. Look at our pit bulls. These are the sweetest pets, but a lot of people automatically think they're vicious killers because of the sensational publicity surrounding the breed. As a black male, I realize how damaging bad publicity can be for any group."

1've always been attracted to black men. Whenever I imagined what my children would look like, I always imagined them of mixed race. There's something intriguing about someone who's different than you. I think a lot of people probably feel the same way I do, but are too timid to act upon it. Funnily enough, Stephen is like my dad in a lot of ways. As the daughter of a Lutheran minister, we moved around the country a lot when I was growing up."

"Which was the opposite from my childhood in Chester, Pennsylvania. I could walk from the house my mom was born in to the house where she died, and I'd have to go by the hospital where I was born to get there! Like most African American Carters in the Philadelphia area, our family came from the Carter plantation in Virginia, which was one of the largest slave holdings in the South. This knowledge wasn't something I discovered as an academic, but was part of our family history that everyone learned as a child. There must have been a path between Virginia and Pennsylvania, because every black Carter I've ever met around the country has ties in Philadelphia, hence Virginia. I was a Catholic altar boy, who for years aspired to the priesthood until I took art classes my senior year in college. I enjoy teaching ceramics at the University of Vermont, even though this part of the country is a rather odd place for a black person to live. Burlington is one of the few places around where the presumption is if you're African American, you probably have a better job than a white person. There basically is no black underclass here. Most blacks were brought in by the university or IBM. There are very few folks of color over twenty that were born here. As of the last census, there were 1,024 African Americans in the entire state. I remember one day this black woman approached me on the sidewalk and asked me, 'Where is the black area?' I laughed and said, 'Well, there are two of us here, so this is it!' It seems like New Englanders have the same polite reserve for everyone, so you never really know their heartfelt attitudes, whereas when I lived in Alabama for

a year, I never had to worry about people stabbing me in the back. If they don't like you, they'll stab you in the heart! At least down South, you always know how you stand with someone. I always say, God help me from white liberals. They're self-satisfied and judgmental."

"When Stephen took his sabbatical, we took the family to Tobago for a year. There our daughter was considered white, whereas here she's black. I felt like my own whiteness put me on a pedestal there."

"One percent of Tobago is white and that's the ninety percent that controls all of the money in that country. The fact that I had a white wife made me look extremely successful in our neighbors' eyes. It was amazing to feel rich on a professor's salary."

"One thing that worries me, as a white mother raising biracial

> "So many people have attributed my tenure to affirmative action. No one seems to notice that I had a 4.0 average through college and graduate school!"

children in Vermont, is that there is no black culture here to expose them to, and that is half their heritage."

"Well, as far as I'm concerned," adds Stephen, "black culture is about the experience of being black in this country, and that's something our kids will certainly experience firsthand, because this nation is far from color-blind. Unfortunately, we live in a society where, if you're black, whatever you do wrong is a reflection of your entire race and whatever you do right is a reflection of the generosity of white society. So many people have attributed my tenure to affirmative action. No one seems to notice that I had a 4.0 average through college and graduate school!"

Growing up as a biracial kid in southern California, I felt free to associate with anyone of any race. My dad's a black police officer and my mom's a white nurse. Dating white girls in high school, I had to put up with some closed-minded stereotypes from some of the parents, but I enjoyed changing people's minds. Once they met me and got to know me, they didn't worry that I was going to steal the silverware or sell drugs on their front lawn! Funnily enough, the worst racism I experienced as a teenager was from black kids, who thought I wasn't 'Black enough.' I refuse to lapse into anyone else's stereotype."

I think that my parents really absorbed the changes brought on by the Civil Rights Movement in the mid-sixties and I've never heard them be racist. As a result, Terry's biracial background wasn't an issue for me or them. I was so oblivious, that Terry was the one that pointed out the disapproving looks we'd sometimes get when we go out together. I probably would never even notice, because being together doesn't feel weird to me."

"Anyone of color is aware that racism is still out there. It's a part of your everyday life, even in a hip place like Seattle, but I still don't believe in using it as an excuse for any of my own failings."

"If I wasn't involved with Terry, I doubt that I'd be aware of the lingering racist attitudes that exist in America. I'd probably just assume that most people feel like I do, that the color of someone's skin is not a marker of their character. There's an invisible line that you're not aware of until you cross it and you see the reactions of other people. There are more lines between us as a people than need be. Black history is a part of American history. It shouldn't be separated from a common legacy that we

all shared in one way or another. How absurd would it be if I studied white history? American history courses should stop being segregated."

"Ebonics is another example of some sort of new age separatism," continues Terry. "It's a staggering example of a good intention having bad results. Every child in America should know correct grammar and punctuation. People judge with their ears as much as their eyes. I know if I'm dressed in a sweat shirt, on the way to racquetball, people are going to treat me differently than if I'm dressed for work. Everyone makes snap judgements on appearances that are about social class as much as they are about race."

Jennifer starts laughing at the memory of the first time she introduced Terry to her grandmother. "She was convinced that Terry was a basketball

> "If I wasn't involved with Terry, I doubt that I'd be aware of the lingering racist attitudes that exist in America. There's an invisible line that you're not aware of until you cross it and you see the reactions of other people."

player and we couldn't dissuade her. She couldn't accept that he was in college just to get an education instead of to be an athlete. Some people don't want to be confused with the facts. Their minds are made up!"

My black dad met my white mom at a jazz club in the late thirties and I arrived in 1942, back in the time when biracial wasn't even a word yet," says Leni. "I always got the question, 'What are you?' or 'What nationality are you?,' which always really irritated me because I felt like it was a trick question. What they really wanted to know was if I'd claim my African American side, or if I was trying to 'pass' into the white community. My mother was very politically active, joining the NAACP when she was seventeen, before she ever met my father. They divorced when I was young and later my mom married a really quite remarkable African American, who with only a third grade education built up an upholstery business. As a young woman, I was in a singing group called The Womenfolk. We performed at the University of Mississippi. It was the first time I'd ever been in the segregated South, where they had no idea that I myself was integrated!"

"I grew up on a family farm in South Dakota and I remember the first time I saw a black man. It scared me because I thought it was the boogie man. I certainly was aware of and resented the racism towards Indians that I saw as a little boy, but it was not nearly as heavy as the racism towards blacks in the South. When I was stationed in Biloxi, Mississippi, in 1955 I experienced institutionalized racism for the first time. I wasn't allowed to go to town with black soldiers from the base, because of the segregation laws there at the time. I was deeply affected by the changing consciousness of the sixties, concerned about equality for all people. Once you step outside of the mainstream, you see things from both sides. Once you do that, it's hard to ever be totally invested in self-interest again."

Leni continues, "There might not be any slave owners still living today, but the white men who killed Emmet Till are still alive, as are the African Americans who had to suffer the indignities of Jim Crow. White folks shouldn't get defensive about this ugly American legacy by saying, 'Well, I didn't do those terrible things.' They should get really angry and say 'Never again'! By 2050, white folks will no longer be a majority in this country, so they better join ranks and make a stand that racism is absolutely intolerable."

"My background as a Scandinavian Lutheran was totally non-racist. My dad was crazy about Leni the first time he met her in 1974. Funnily enough, he'd experienced racism against himself, being a Dane in a Norwegian and Swedish community. It seems like every group always needs another group to blame their problems on."

"The first day I met his dad, he used the word 'nigger.' I took him aside and said, 'Nels, if you want to describe people of African descent, you have to use some other word, because that one is too hurtful to me.' He had no idea how insulting that word can be to a people struggling for equal rights because he's always lived in a place where there simply weren't any blacks. I never heard him say that word again and both of Kip's parents were

> "My pet peeve is people using that old saw against mixed marriage, 'What about the children?' Well, I'm one of those children. What am I supposed to do, just curl up and die? Never have children, so I won't 'contaminate' their blood?"

wonderful in-laws. They loved us because we moved on to their South Dakota homestead, where we gardened, cleaned fish and milked cows—all the things that no one else wanted to do any longer! Both our daughter, Winter, and our son, Bjorn, were born there, as was Nels."

"Now we're living in Brown's Cove, with more of a history of segregation. We're outside of the protective umbrella of my extended family, and although Leni and I haven't had any problems with prejudice, we weren't always able to protect our kids. Race has nothing to do with my relationship with Leni. The only time I ever think about it

is when something comes from outside. Our kids have had to put up with mess at school."

Leni turns to her kids, Bjorn and Winter, and says, "Like the kids on the bus who called you white African nigger lips."

"They never used the term African," says Bjorn. "I doubt they knew where Africa is, but they sure knew how to recognize a nigger!"

"Living deep in the country," says his sister, Winter, "the kids around here are suspicious. They used to call me a white nigger lesbian."

"When they came home from school with these stories of being called quarter breeds or worse," adds Leni, "it just blew me away. I certainly had never experienced that sort of hostility growing up, and I was born in 1942!"

"Bjorn and I started high school in ninth and tenth grade, after being home schooled," says Winter, "and it was quite a shock. They called us all kinds of names. I remember my first year there, a girl asked me if I was 'mixed with something.' It was the first time I'd ever thought about my

> "I've got relatives that traveled with Lewis and Clark and my great grandfather was born a slave. I'm a true American."

race. It's fascinating to realize that, as fair skinned as I am, I'm as much part Negro as Thomas Jefferson's slave, Sally Hemings."

"The bus drivers were no help. Sometimes they'd even join in. These kids were eighteen years old and four hundred pounds of beef in ninth grade. There was certainly nothing Winter and I could do except pity them. When I grew tall and started dressing in black, they stopped messing with me. I think they thought I worshiped Satan, which was fine with me because it made them afraid to talk to me!"

"One sad thing to realize," adds Kip, " is that for a lot of kids on that school bus, it's the only time in thier lives that they'll ever be able to feel superior. Nothing much happens for them after they get out of school, except a dead-end job that can disappear anytime."

"I think racism is a really big deal in high school. Because we look white," says Winter, "Bjorn and I hear all kinds of racist slurs that brown skin folks wouldn't be privy to. It's really upsetting. These kids are just repeating what they heard somewhere else. They didn't invent these attitudes. It's not just white folks that are race obsessed. When Mom took Bjorn and me to her family reunion, we were the only really pale kids there and some of our cousins had no problem telling us that we didn't 'belong'."

"The first thing I did when we got home," says Leni, "is show the kids a picture of Walter White, one of the early leaders of the NAACP."

Winter continues, "He's a blue-eyed blond African American, just like me, and he became my spiritual mentor growing up. Every individual can make the world a better place by their own actions. I will never stand silent when I experience bigotry. Like Walter White, I can see and hear things that are hidden from my dark skin relatives, and it's my vow to stand up for what's right and fair."

"My pet peeve is people using that old saw against mixed marriage, 'What about the children?' says Leni. "Well, I'm one of those children. What am I supposed to do, just curl up and die? Never have children, so I won't 'contaminate' their blood?"

Winter jumps in, "My main pet peeve in the world is when you have to identify your race on a form. I always check 'black', because legally I can, so I might as well prove how ridiculous the whole concept is. I never check 'other'. Everybody's mixed with something else. As a country, we need to get over this obsession with race."

Her mother, Leni, says, " I hope that the polarity of having to choose fades away as a growing pain. I hope our culture swings back to the idea that people of any shade can be considered American first, instead of Afro-Americans. It seems like that terminology is some new form of segregation. Black history, art and literature in the United States should be considered American, without any extra tag to differentiate it from other ethnic groups. I've got relatives that traveled with Lewis and Clark and my great grandfather was born a slave. I'm a true American. Remember, the original hominoid tribe that migrated out of Africa 100,000 years ago forms the genetic base for everyone on the planet. There is no 'other.' We're all related."

We met at a party at Brown, where Veronica was a student. I'd just been commissioned as an ensign in the Navy and sent to Rhode Island for school. We hit it off right away and exchanged phone numbers. A few months later, I was stationed in Norfolk, Virginia, so we had a ten hour drive to see each other on the weekends."

"*We got married the summer after I graduated. The two families got along great at the wedding.*"

"Her parents are from the Bronx and had no idea what life in the South was really like, except what was shown on television, which was usually not a positive depiction."

"*Growing up in my neighborhood in New York was like growing up in the Caribbean. Jamaicans, Puerto Ricans, Dominicans, Haitians—a rainbow of race and culture. It was a very different world than the Deep South, where there are two races, black and white, and they are pretty much separated. I don't think Donald knew quite what to make of me when we first met.*"

"Veronica was the first person I'd ever dated who wasn't African American. The fact that her skin was paler than mine wasn't an issue because most black families have a spectrum of color, but I wasn't used to being with someone who didn't identify with being black or white. Where I come from, everyone had a strong racial identity one way or the other. You basically lived on one side of the tracks or the other. When the two of us visit Georgia together, I can see folks looking at Veronica and trying to figure out if she's white or black. My sister is very light skinned and I'm dark. It really bothered me when I was little. Living in a racist society, I felt that lighter was better. As I grew older, and became more educated about racism, I realized that light skin does not equal superiority."

"*All people of color share a common background of slave trade and colonization that resulted in miscegenation, through force or otherwise, so as a Puerto Rican, I certainly identify with African Americans more than*

a European would. Being a student at Brown reinforced in me a desire to identify closely with oppressed cultures and races."

"In American society, if an African American messes up, people tend to form negative perceptions of an entire race from the actions of that one person, but if we do things right, we're often looked at as an individual exception. The military is a reflection of society, and racism is alive and well within the ranks. We should not be misled by the success of a few. With so few senior black officers to share their stories, many young black officers can't identify pitfalls and career enhancing opportunities when they come along. I think this is why so many African American officers fail to be selected for advancement. While mentoring should be color-blind, cultural differences sometimes make it harder for senior white officers

> "Race, as we understand it, is an artificial economic and social term designed to enforce slavery. The 'one drop rule' was a law invented to keep the growing mulatto population in the slave pool."

and young black officers to identify with each other."

"*As a history teacher, my main focus of interest is the legacy of the 'one drop rule' and the whole idea of race categories. One concern surrounding the subject of race is the science of its very existence. Race, as we understand it, is an artificial economic and social term that came into being to enforce slavery. The 'one drop rule' was a law invented to keep the growing mulatto population in the slave pool. With the growing numbers of racially, culturally, and ethnically mixed children, the categories we cling to are severely outdated. We need to revolutionize our perceptions of ourselves and each other.*"

We met when we were both working for a large printing company. We had a mutual best friend that we socialized with all the time, so that's how we first started spending time together after work."

"Ron was very protective of people finding out that we were dating, because he was afraid that white guys might not want to go out with me if they found out that I was dating him. We kept quiet about it for quite some time. I was more than a little nervous about what my family would say, as well. Dating outside of our race wasn't anything we were used to."

"My grandmother was white," says Ron, "so I certainly wasn't uncomfortable personally with the idea of racial mixing. In fact, all six of my white grandmother's sisters and brothers married black people. Back then, an entire family would be rejected by the white community if you crossed the color line, so my grandmother and her siblings joined the black community, where they were accepted. They called themselves black. About the only time my grandmother would go back into the white part of town was when she went to the hairdresser, and then she'd be dropped off several blocks away, so the beautician wouldn't see her riding around in the car with blacks. She was afraid that they wouldn't fix her hair. So you can see why I was a little protective of Suzanne when we first started seeing each other. Looking back thirteen years ago, I think her parents' friends looked at Suzanne's love for me as some act of rebellion, like something she was 'doing' to her parents."

"If my relationship with Ron has 'done' anything to my parents, it's only been a positive experience. Time has taught them what a good husband and father to their grandchildren he is and they've always liked his whole family. My parents have told me that they've learned so much from seeing the two of us together, what's important and what's not. You should be at our house over the holidays, when both of our families are here."

"Black or white, it's the same—the women are running around doing all the cooking and all the cleaning, while the men are snoozing on the sofa in front of the ball game! And the kids, well, kids are just kids."

"At the beginning, though, it was a big thing in the small town where I grew up, when the news broke about Ron and me getting engaged to be married. I learned very quickly who my friends weren't. I got dropped like that (she snaps her fingers). My dad said people would come up to him at work with condolences, like something really terrible had happened to his daughter. People in our church were all concerned, but our minister was always supportive of us. Because both Ron and I are Methodist, he'd tell people that he was so glad it wasn't a mixed marriage! The biggest difference between Black and White America is the churches. Ron is still the only black member of the congregation. It's the last stronghold of segregation."

"I still like to go to the black church. There's nothing like the

> "It's like he was Ron, the co-worker and ball player until he crossed that line and dated a white woman, then he was a nigger."

preaching and gospel music there. We take the kids to Suzanne's church, because there are more activities there for children. The main concern I've had, as far as being an interracial couple, is for our kids—how they'll be treated. Every parent feels protective of their children, and we're no different. My secret fear is that they'll be ashamed for me to come to their school, because the kids will tease them. It's never happened, but I used to worry about it. The reality is, once people get to know us as a couple, no one even notices or thinks about the fact that we're a biracial family."

"Most white people have no idea about the daily acts of subtle discrimination that black Americans have to deal with. If I go in a store and write a check, no one even asks me for identification. But if I'm with Ron, I have to show two different ones."

"During the O.J. Simpson trial a few years ago, it really shook me up that there was such distrust between the races, but as a black man, I have to say that I could understand the small victory of having the tables of justice turned. Sometimes it seems like racial equality is just a fragile surface on America, without much depth. For example, my mother felt the need to console us because our second child was dark skinned when he was born. 'Don't worry, he'll get lighter,' she said. There was a man at work who I used to play baseball with, and we got along fine until I started dating Suzanne. Then he was saying, 'Can you believe Suzanne is dating that nigger?'"

"It's like he was Ron, the co-worker and ball player until he crossed that line and dated a white woman, then he was a nigger. The stereotypes that some people have about mixed marriages take me by surprise sometime. One of our son's teachers said to me, 'You must have had it so hard,' and I'm like, 'Excuse me?' Ron and I have built a wonderful life together. If anything, we feel fortunate. Sure, we've had some neighbors not speak to us, including Ron's old baseball and

> "Our minister was always supportive of us. Because both Ron and I are Methodist, he'd tell people that he was so glad it wasn't a mixed marriage!"

football coach, who did not approve of us, especially us living in his neighborhood!"

"That kind of hurt me. What's scary is he works in the public school system, so you can see why we feel protective of our kids. Hopefully, when our kids have kids, these worries won't even enter their minds."

"Until I met Ron, I'd never met a man who could fill my dad's shoes. So I prayed about it, and asked Him to send me a man who will love me and that I can count on, and it didn't occur to me to specify his color, so He sent me Ron. So obviously race is not an issue with God, even if it gets people's attention. I've had people ask me if my son was 'foreign' or assume that I was black and ask me why my other son was so white! I just say, 'I just don't know, you'd have to ask God!'"

When we bought this house, we made a conscious decision to live in a African American neighborhood," says Maurice, in the large, formal front parlor of his colonial revival home. "I wanted my family to be exposed to the roots of the black community and we found that they run deep here. This end of Ridge Street used to be all white until a black man named George Ferguson bought this home. He was the first to break the color line and there was almost immediate 'white flight'. This house has seen a cross burned in its front yard and bricks tossed through its windows. Still today, this town is very much segregated. My work environment is predominately white, so coming home to Ridge Street is my own way of reconnecting with my folk. After ten years of adapting to my wife's culture in Italy, I wanted to re-establish ties with my African American heritage and introduce my community to my wife and children. A tragic result of integration in this country was that most black middle class professionals abandoned our black neighborhoods. I dare say that until we moved into this house, the kids growing up around here rarely saw a black man walking these streets with a briefcase in his hand. I'm sure some of my friends look at moving into this area as self-segregation, but I look at it as a simple and conscious affirmation of my heritage."

"We don't look at our home as purely a financial investment. It's more important to us that we invest in a community we care about. If we don't make money on it—big deal. We'll have no regrets, because we did the right thing. Since my high school days in Florence, I've always been involved in political groups that work toward making things better for the under-represented, so it was perfectly natural for me to be an advocate for the African American community when we moved to America. My own political heritage is very much about soul-stirring 'power to the people.' Maurice and I met in Florence in 1980, while he was still a student in architecture and I was early in my architectural practice. He was the first black man I ever met. It was a time in my life when I didn't want to be

romantically involved, so Maurice seemed safe, because he was from a different culture, another country, another color. I let down my defenses around him because there were so many differences between us—and that's what got me, because I was totally open to him. I also remember stories that my mother told me when I was a little girl about how the African American soldiers came into to her small village in Italy at the end of World War II to bring them freedom and end the war. So in my mind, I'd always had this heroic idea of black people. Also, politically, I was always on their side, always admiring of America's civil rights leaders like Martin Luther King and Malcolm X. I also admired the white Americans who didn't get mired down in guilt over the inequality."

"At her school, the black kids accuse her of 'acting white' because she excels academically and likes art, but she isn't offended by the accusation, because her mother is white."

"Giovanna's friends were all pretty far left politically and identified with the underdog, so I was instantly embraced in their circle. Because Italians don't have much racial diversity in their country, they are free of the prejudices that Americans have. I never had any sense of being treated as inferior because of my skin color in all the years I lived there. My blackness certainly wasn't a demerit, like it is here. Of course, they don't have the legacy of the trans Atlantic African slave trade, so why would they share the same mental muddle as Americans? I spent most of my twenties in Italy, and unlike growing up in America, my race was rarely an issue. Until I met Giovanna, I'd never been romantically involved with any white women. It never even occurred to me. In high school I was downright militant, involved in politically charged street theater that aggressively addressed African American issues, so falling in love with Giovanna was quite a departure for me. I, too, think I was totally opened and let my guard down around her because I didn't think of her as a potential girlfriend. After spending a decade in Florence, it was a shock to have to readjust to race as a daily issue when we moved to America. For example, as a taxpayer, I feel entitled to the same services from the city in this neighborhood as I would living in any other part of town, but it's a constant struggle to achieve that equality. Now that I'm involved in local politics, I find myself always having to look through the race lens. It's an unhappy reality that so many decisions are tinted by misperception and racial prejudice. While I realize that much of the subtext of many issues is race, whether it's city/county reversion, or who's elected sheriff, I don't make my decisions solely on race, though it's very much a factor. It's a constant struggle for me to be the strongest advocate I can be for the

> "A tragic result of integration in this country was that most black middle class professionals abandoned our black neighborhoods. I'm sure some of my friends look at moving into a black neighborhood as self-segregation, but I look at it as a simple and conscious affirmation of my heritage."

African American community and at the same time support decisions that are best for the entire town."

"After living all my life in Florence, it was a difficult transition to be living in an American town. The same is true for our kids. Our son refused to speak English for the first two years we were here. I tend to still speak Italian around the dinner table, but Maurice and the two kids usually will answer me in English. Language wasn't as much of an adjustment as adapting to life in a rather small town, after being total urbanites for years in Florence. Living here has been a real eye opener. I'm more aware of both people's similarities and differences."

"Our kids are really the main reason I wanted to move back to America. I wanted them to see black people who were doing things other than selling fake Gucci pocketbooks on the street in Florence. They had no perception of their African American heritage and American culture other than through me, and I was becoming Italian myself."

"Bringing them to the United States was important to me as well. Everything I've ever read about biracial children says it's important to expose them to both sides of their inheritance. They belong to both worlds and should understand the richness of America as well as Europe."

"At this point, they realize that their tastes are different from most kids their age. Our daughter loves classical music much more than rap or rock, because that's what she was exposed to in Italy. So it's interesting to realize that so many of the differences between people are simply learned behaviors. At her school, the black kids accuse her of 'acting white' because she excels academically and likes art, but she isn't offended by the accusation, because her mother is white..."

"...so her reaction is like 'So what?'" laughs Giovanna. "The way that she walks and talks, actually occupies space, is different from most of her African American peers at school. I think returning to America has made her appreciate her European upbringing and hopefully living here will give her greater access to her African American heritage."

"I've come to the realization that I don't want my kids to ever be 'cool,'" confides Maurice. "I see little five-year-olds who are already tougher than I'd ever want my son to be. Being 'hard' just closes you off from learning. In the end, we try to teach our kids that it's better to be smart than to be cool. When I think about the bond between Giovanna and me, our mutual love of light, color, and form, how we can walk down the street and enjoy the hue of the sunlight reflecting off a building, that's what we want for our children—for them to be as aware as possible of the world around them. It's been my experience that if you take time to get to know someone, the prejudice you may have towards them tends to fall apart. Our kids are lucky in that they get an inside look at both the black and white community and our respective cultures. It's important to acknowledge and respect each other's cultures so we can successfully navigate through different worlds. The good, the bad, the ugly is all part of life and you can't sanitize it or scrub it completely clean without creating a sterile, unreal, environment. Seventy-five percent of my architecture students have never even been to a great city. The creation of cities is one of man's greatest achievements, but they've grown up on suburban cul-de-sacs and know nothing of the exciting, volatile diversity of urbanity."

W e're both from Pennsylvania, but we met at college, while I was in my first year and Rob was in his last," says Sandy, as she nurses their three-month-old son.

"We were both jocks in the weight room," laughs Rob. "It was just starting to dawn on me that I wouldn't be in school forever and I'd better start taking my life a little more seriously. The first time I saw Sandy, I thought, 'Now there's something I could be serious about.'"

"When he asked me out, I was taken aback because even though I'd always run track and had tons of African American friends, it was the first time a black guy had ever asked me out on a date. When I went back to my dorm and asked my friends if I should go out with him, they said 'Sure, you're not going to marry the guy!'"

"I know this sounds strange, but even on our first date, I could very easily imagine being married to Sandy. When we were introduced in the gym, as we were shaking hands, a voice in my head said, 'You guys are going to get married.' How strange is that? Her race was simply a non-issue for me, as I'd dated just as many white girls as I had black by the time we met. It's hard to believe that was fourteen years ago."

"Our fifth wedding anniversary is coming up soon. For years when we were dating, I kept it a secret from my parents. They had never specifically said I should never date a black man but I intuitively knew they'd hate the idea, even though I never remember them saying racist remarks while I was growing up."

"Who can blame them for being suspicious of blacks? I mean, if you don't really know any African Americans personally, and your only contact with the race is through what you see on the TV and the movies, or what you read in newspapers and magazines, what are you going to think? Samuel Jackson, with a gun! Even blacks are affected by our negative image in the media. When I see a brother in a hooded sweatshirt, I have a moment's anxiety. That's why the Million Man March on Washington was so important for African Americans' self-image. It went

against the stereotype of irresponsibility and violence. My parents raised me to be twice as good in everything I did, in order to combat racist stereotypes."

"It seems silly now, but I broke up with Rob because of my parents' anxiety over the two of us being together. It was incredibly painful all the way around and ultimately impossible for us to stay apart—thanks to Rob's persistence that we really belonged together."

"Not that I didn't sometimes have my own moments of guilt, that I shouldn't marry white, in order to have a black family. Why, I'm not really sure. My parents never preached anything like that."

"What was really painful for me was my mother's reaction that my love for Rob was something I was doing to spite her. Nothing could have been

> "Often, when people marry outside their race, others will argue against it by saying, 'What about the children?' Well, what about the children? There's nothing not to like here."

further from the truth. I really wanted her blessing, not her disapproval. Tears were just streaming down her face as she asked me, 'Why are you stabbing me in the back?'"

"In my mother-in-law's defense, this was before she ever met me. She didn't know any black people, so of course there was a fear of the unknown."

"One of the beautiful things about our marriage is the positive ripple effect we've had on not only my immediate family, but our cousins and friends as well. One of the things my dad really admires in a person is the ability to work hard and once he got to see that quality in Rob, his attitude

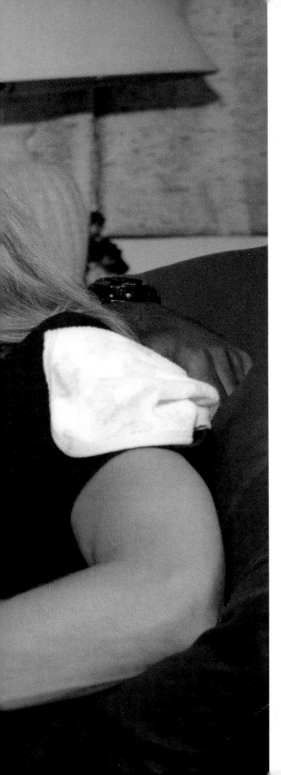

towards him changed."

"*At our wedding he gave the nicest toast about how he was happy for our marriage because he knew we were hard workers and that we'd build a good life for ourselves. Since the baby's been born, I can't believe how loving her parents have become towards me. It's amazing, really, when you think that we used to pretend like our relationship didn't exist, and now we just wish we could see more of her parents all the time. I know they really like me and see that Sandy and I make each other happy. It's not just the two of us anymore. Her parents and mine have become close and both equally love their grandson. Once Sandy's parents accepted me, I felt totally embraced. And I'm sure Sandy doesn't look like the daughter-in-law my mother expected to have when I was growing up, but now we all feel like family.*"

"All the pain and anxiety of our first years together are just a distant memory now. I'm still a little bit intimidated to be a white woman raising a biracial son in a world that is often racist, but I have faith that Rob and I will be able to see him through. I mean, you have to believe in yourselves. No one, no matter who they are, has any guarantees that everything will be easy."

"*We broke up more than once when we were dating over the anxiety of marrying outside of our race, but that stress was a good thing because it made us realize what's really important.*"

"You have to make decisions based on what you believe in more than trying to please others. Eventually, I came to realize that I really believed in us as a couple—that we shared the same values and would be able to handle things as they came up."

"*Yes, everyone has their own things to deal with. I mean, if our kid grows to be a big guy, kids are a lot less likely to call him names than*

"When I went back to my dorm and asked my friends if I should go out with him, they said 'Sure, you're not going to marry the guy!'"

if he was small."

"Well, what sort of things do you think they'd call him?" asks Sandy.

"*Nothing worse than anything I've ever heard!*" laughs Rob as he kisses his son on the top of his head. "*You should see our baby's grandparents with him. He is one well-loved child. Often, when people marry outside their race, others will argue against it by saying, 'What about the children?' Well, what about the children? There's nothing not to like here. And if someone else's child is so ignorant that they call people names, well that's their problem more than ours. I believe love goes over, around, and beyond anything you put in its way and you have to be true to your heart.*"

1 had visited Jamaica a number of times on vacation," says Carlotta in her warm, fragrant kitchen, "and about five or six years ago I went down there to live for a while, because I loved it so much. Biff had a shop of his woodcarvings in the craft market there, so I saw him almost daily on the way to the beach. We became lovers when I moved down there and we moved in together. When I had to go back to the States after six months, because of Jamaican immigration laws, we knew we wanted to keep our relationship going somehow."

"I got to know lots of tourists because of my shop," says Biff in his lilting Jamaican accent, "but I was never a 'rent-a Rasta'—I'd never had a white girlfriend before. Like all Jamaicans, I'd thought about coming to the United States, but I never really thought I'd live here. Tourism is about the only industry in my country, so everyone meets people from all over the world and that makes us curious about other parts of the world."

"We realized when we were apart that we wanted to stay together, but the only way for him to get to this country was on a fiancée visa, which gives you ninety days to get married or go back. My parents were probably hoping it was just a vacation fling, but they were more concerned about his ability to support me, as opposed to me initially having to support him, than his race."

"Some of my friends would say it wasn't right to be with a white woman, but I think if they had the opportunity to date Carlotta, they would! I'm a Rastafarian and we believe in equal rights and unity for all people. There is only one God, which all people worship under a different name. I think everyone is one people. It's no matter, black or white, we are still one. Unity is strength. Until we all realize this, there are always going to be problems on this earth."

"The whole race issue, living in Jamaica, was much less apparent than living in this country. I would go places with Biff where there were no other whites at all, and it wouldn't be the least bit uncomfortable. In America, you would almost certainly feel more out-of-place in a similar situation. I think Biff has a different experience in America as a black man because he's Jamaican. Everyone wants to approach him and talk to him, which is certainly not the case for most African Americans."

"Where I come from, people don't have to make excuses for their color. The first time I come up against this racist attitude is when I go to get my Virginia driver's license. The white man behind the counter obviously did not like my face."

"I went up and tried to help, it only built up a bigger wall of resistance. He just did not want to give him a license. Poor Biff had no idea how to use a computer and they weren't about to help him. He persevered and I don't think they could believe when he finally got it."

"I've got to really drive carefully, because they can deport me if I get a

> "I think Biff has a different experience in America as a black man because he's Jamaican. Everyone wants to approach him and talk to him, which is certainly not the case for most African Americans."

speeding ticket. Not that I don't want to go back to Jamaica one day, but right now, we can make more money here. Everybody in America works so hard, all the time. There's not enough time to get to know each other by just hanging out together."

"One thing that's neat about our neighborhood is that it's very racially mixed. It's a funny coincidence, but there are three mixed couples in a row in our cul-de-sac." Carlotta pauses thoughtfully, then adds, "I don't think our different races has been much of an issue in our life together. We just feel like us, whether we're going to a Contra dance or a Reggae show."

My father graduated at the top of his class from the university in Akron, Ohio with a master's degree in chemistry, but Goodyear didn't hire black chemists, so he worked as an elevator operator, ferrying his fellow classmates up and down for years," says Rita. "Finally, a former professor of his convinced Goodyear to hire him, and my dad was the first black chemist in the rubber industry. When I was in second grade, we were the first black family to move into this white neighborhood, where we experienced 'white flight' firsthand. By high school, there was only one white family left, appropriately enough named the Browns. As far as school was concerned, I honestly can't remember much racial animosity or even tension at all. I remember listening to the speeches of Stokely Carmichael, Malcolm X, and Martin Luther King; however, most of the white kids in my class of 1970 also supported their ideals too. My family marched on Washington, but that was also an integrated experience. The assassinations of Martin Luther King and Robert Kennedy were tragedies that brought black and white students together, not apart. There was, however, an invisible line between the races when it came to dating. I remember my mother telling me that the more education I got, the harder it would be for me to find an African American man. My world has become progressively 'whiter' over the years, so by the time I was in graduate school, I was quite often the only black person in the room."

"We met in 1976 when I was a fellow in the University of Iowa's International Writing Program and she was in graduate school at the Iowa Writer's Workshop," says Fred. "She was one of the first people I met when I arrived from Germany, because she was my translator. I had written my lecture in German, and she translated it into English. I was immediately attracted to her."

"I was completely taken by his lack of self-consciousness about our racial differences. I'd dated white guys before, and it was usually fraught with a nervousness that was entirely lacking when I was with Fred."

"Well, my generation in Germany emphatically rejected the idea of racial and ethnic 'purity' after the racist Nazi horrors, so I had no sense that races should be separate."

"It's funny how things work out. I studied German since junior high school, probably because most kids took French, so I wanted to do something different. By the time I graduated from college, I had enough German language credits to get a Fulbright Scholarship to study in Germany for a year, and that's why I was qualified to be Fred's translator. It's like I'd been preparing throughout my school years to meet Fred!"

"My first novel, published in Germany in 1969, was titled Die Schwarzen Tauben, which means 'The Black Doves', so talk about curious coincidence! It does make you wonder if some things were meant to be. My

> "As a kid, I was always very conscious that there was an official history that they taught in school, then there were things that everyone in the neighborhood knew were true."

own family was in many ways as unusual as Rita's. My father was the first person in the family to go to school beyond eighth grade. To go to America was the dream of many kids in Germany when I was growing up. The German student movement started getting really involved in anti-Vietnam War protests, motivated in part by people like Herbert Marcuse at Berkeley, whose philosophical reasoning had also helped to get the American students mobilized."

"Angela Davis studied with Marcuse in California, then went to graduate school in Frankfurt, so there was a complex connection between German philosophers and the worldwide student protest movement," adds Rita.

"We were quite a seventies couple, in my old rusted out LTD station wagon, with Rita's mattress in the back, traveling across the country. Her poor parents when we showed up at 7:00 a.m. in this beat up old car with a mattress in the back! They were quite conservative in that respect, but her mother never mentioned the fact that we seemed to be sharing a bed or that I was a different race. We'd purposely timed the visit when her dad would be at work, because we were more than a little nervous what his reaction would be on both counts. When he finally did meet me, he adopted a kind of 'don't ask, don't tell' policy."

"Eventually they became upset that we were living together without being married, and race wasn't much of an issue in comparison. My dad stopped speaking to me for a while as a sign of his disapproval."

"And the really weird thing is he kept being perfectly cordial to me, even though he wouldn't speak to Rita."

> "As a poet, I've always carried this sense of an unspoken history, a sense of voices that are silent, a need to make sure that things are not forgotten or glossed over."

"All this became old news after we got married in 1979, before we moved to Berlin. When our daughter was born in January 1983, we were both surprised to have this little blue-eyed blond. She looked like a German Gerber baby. Over the years her eyes have turned gray and her hair has gotten darker, but she is a true citizen of the world, as comfortable with her black relatives in Ohio as she is with her white classmates in college. She has both American and German citizenship, and we've raised her bilingual."

"Now, Rita's great grandmother was an Irishwoman who married a Blackfoot Indian, so like most African Americans, light skin and eyes are not uncommon in her family."

"A geneticist would have lots of fun studying our DNA. My dad almost looks Asian, or Native American, while my mom is pretty dark skinned. I was so delighted when the whole Sally Hemings/Thomas Jefferson affair was finally proven through scientific testing. Why is it so hard for some people to deal with the fact that he fathered her children? Human relations are very complicated. Slavery or not, the nature of men and women is basically the same today as it was two hundred years ago. As a poet, I've always carried this sense of an unspoken history, a sense of voices that are silent, a need to make sure that things are not forgotten or glossed over. Even as a kid, I was always very conscious that there was an official history that they taught in school, then there were things that everyone in the neighborhood knew were true. Even though it's not illegal for Fred and me to be together as a couple, as it still was in some states a mere thirty-some years ago, we're not unaware that some people might not approve."

"We've been together for twenty-five years now, and we've experienced very little harassment as an interracial couple. As a long-haired hippie, I was so used to being stared at, that I didn't really notice much difference when Rita and I got together, except in Alabama, where people would sometimes give us the evil eye, just glare at us."

"In 1982, we lived in Auburn, Alabama, and that was definitely not a place where a mixed couple could always feel accepted—at least not off the university campus. Once our tires were slashed while we were grocery shopping. We used to have to drive by this fraternity that had a huge confederate flag hanging out front."

"This is the same fraternity that used to give plantation parties, where they'd hire blacks to dress up as slaves and serve drinks to hoop-skirted guests."

"Once when we drove by, the frat boys started pelting our car windshield with snowballs and surrounded our car."

"It definitely felt like a mob, which doesn't bring out the best aspects of humanity. When I heard someone yell 'nigger!' I felt like I could justify stepping on the gas, even if they were blocking the way. There were a dozen, maybe fifteen, guys surrounding us, and I knew our best hope was to keep the car moving. To this day, it's very vivid in my mind, like a movie scene."

"Later, we talked about what to do with that kind of hate," says Rita. "If I become bitter and angry, then I've let the bad guys win. They've made me become more like them, and that's absolutely not something I want to do. We were both raised to believe in positive values and betterment."

"Which is absolutely true, but the exceptions push themselves in the foreground and make the most noise, so we just have to remind ourselves that hateful people are not the majority," continues Fred.

"I remember walking along a park in Queens at night on the way from the subway back to a friend's apartment, and being surrounded by a gang of black teenagers. They took Fred's cowboy hat off his head and were joking around, obviously with the intent of intimidating us, or even more sinister ambitions. Fred just joked back and seemed unfazed. When we finally reached our friend's apartment, the leader says, 'Take my advice, don't walk through here at night,' and Fred said, 'Thanks... now can I get my hat back?' Which he did. I could tell that these kids were impressed that Fred did not have the standard reactions to them as they apprehended us. He treated them respectfully, as fellow human beings. We have to remember, for kids in that neighborhood, the only recourse that society leaves them to feel any sense of power or mastery, is to make others feel afraid. But I think they really appreciated not scaring us that night."

1t's easier for black families to accept interracial marriage, because any children from that union will be considered black. It's more difficult for white parents to accept that their grandchildren will be a different race. In our case, though, I think Theresa's family was more accepting of our relationship than my folks, probably because I was the only son, and my dad was minister of a church which was the center of a black community."

I don't think I was exactly the ideal daughter-in-law that your dad had in mind," laughs Theresa.

"Despite my parent's initial feelings of anxiety, over time they've accepted Theresa as part of the Scruggs clan. When my father's mother died, Daddy wanted Theresa to sing at the funeral, which revealed to me that he was making a strong effort to include her in our family. Recently, our parents have been getting together on their own for no reason, except to enjoy each other's company. In our time together, we've seen great changes in attitude and that has brought about great changes in behavior. One area we, as a couple, haven't been able to settle is finding a church we can attend as a family—one that is diverse. Someone said that the most segregated hour in America is eleven o'clock Sunday morning. From a historical perspective, black churches were incredibly important in forming the foundations of black culture in this country. In the time of slavery, they were the only places where blacks were allowed to congregate. Even today, we tend to go on all day long. It's a place where a man who's a janitor during the week can get cleaned up and be chairman of the deacon board. A lady who's a washerwoman can put on her best clothes and be a star soloist. For years, church has been the place where black people can feel good about themselves. They might be ignored or even mistreated all week, but on Sunday morning they could stand up and speak their minds and be listened to with respect. It was the first place where black Americans had a voice."

"Church is one area where there's been little integration," Theresa

confirms. "Schools, neighborhoods, and the workplace are much more integrated. There you see a lot of change."

"I see change too, but some of it isn't so good," continues Horace, who teaches music in high school. "I see kids get disrespected by their classmates if they make good grades, or get a job after school. It's sad, really. It's been a terrible thing for the black community that the values of hard work and honesty are perceived as 'white values' and therefore less desirable. In my day, achievement wasn't a 'white value.'"

"It's so frustrating for him, because he tries to instill worthwhile goals in his students, but their home life holds them back. When our daughter, Hannah, was born, we gave up a lot of income for me to stay at home, but someone has to look after our children and I think a child's parents owe

> "One area we, as a couple, haven't been able to settle, is finding a church we can attend as a family—one that is diverse."

them that. It's not that kids are so much worse than we were, it's just that we've taken the guard rails away and they're left on their own at a time when they still need guidance and supervision. This goes for white kids as well as black."

"It's important to talk about the differences between the races because it promotes understanding, and therefore respect. In black culture, we're spontaneous and enthusiastic, like in our churches. That may spill over to the way we walk down the street, or talk in a movie theater, but it doesn't mean we're hostile or rude. It just means that we have different cultural traditions. How could we not, after hundreds of years of segregation? We had to improvise—not only our religious ceremonies, but our music, or storytelling—our whole way of life."

When I grew up in Metuchen, New Jersey, it was a small, progressive town with a school system that was ranked one of the best in the state," says Julian. "Its slogan was 'The Brainy Borough.' Even though it was only thirty-five miles outside of New York City, it never felt like a bedroom community that emptied out during working hours. In my day the schools were always integrated, but the neighborhoods were fairly segregated. Our street was unusual in that there were both races living on the same street, but there certainly weren't any interracial families that I can remember."

"Logan County, West Virginia was a whole different world. It was coal mining country, and I don't think our public schools were known for their excellence! Both my neighborhood and elementary school were all white, so I was completely isolated from blacks when I was a little girl. Julian and I got to know each other while working in the same office in Washington."

"It definitely started out as a friendship. We were both in other relationships when we met. Beverly had been in D.C. for a while, and I was still going back to New York every weekend."

"He never did like Washington very much, while I really liked it. I'd never even had a close friend who wasn't white, but Julian had lots of friends of both races, and had often dated white women. I respected him as a colleague, but was in denial that my feelings ran deeper than that."

"You have to realize that I worked in Europe from '75 until '81, so I was used to dating different nationalities."

"Yeah, though they were all the glamour girl type. When I finally admitted to myself that my feelings for Julian weren't entirely professional, I was disturbed, because I knew my family wouldn't approve of the relationship. When we started dating, I kept it from them for a long time. Even after we were married, it took them years to accept us as a couple. I don't think Julian's parents were thrilled over me either, at first. The funny thing is, even though I wasn't like the high fashion type that he usually dated, I'm a lot like his mother. We're both quiet and restrained—a little bit corny and old fashioned."

"After a few years of being rejected by her family, I pretty much gave her an ultimatum. Beverly had to choose between me and her parents—either get married, or break up."

"It really tore me up that their initial attitude toward Julian was based on fear and ignorance. I know it hurt him, even though their attitude was so irrational that it wasn't even personal. Mother came to accept him long before Dad was able to re-adjust his expectations. I think, in general, mothers are more accepting of their children's exploits. In hindsight, I see that Julian's instinct to get married was correct—you have to push the envelope to make things change. My dad was never going to accept us as a couple if we kept waiting for his approval. I counsel young interracial couples today by telling them they can't wait for the approval of others—they've got to lead the way. When Daddy died a few years ago, it was Julian who was holding his hand at his bedside. Their relationship is proof that change is possible."

"We are still inherently a racist country, and the only way to breach the separation between blacks and whites is to acknowledge that the division exists and work from there. You certainly can't fix a problem if you don't admit you have one."

"Because we got married late in life, we chose not to have children..."

"...and I regret that, because Julian has always said that the world should be filled with café au lait-colored children. Then we wouldn't have race relations problems."

"Ironically, after such a rocky start we've become the primary caretakers of our parents now that they're getting on in years. Her father never could bring himself to apologize for all those years of rejection..."

"...no, instead, he constructed this event that would invite us to West Virginia. He called and said, 'You and your sister have been good girls, so I want you and your husbands to come to your mother's furrier in Charleston

and pick out a fur coat.' After that, there was never any reserve coming from my parents. We were just expected to get together during the holidays..."

"...and there was never any conversation about all those years when he wouldn't speak to me."

"Well, our family is quite repressed. My parents are not very good at talking about their feelings. I think most of their generation is like that."

"Well, I think you should just have a good argument and get over it!," laughs Julian. "White folks act funny sometimes. You should see the way women clutch their purses when I walk by. It doesn't matter if I have on a coat and tie, jewelry stores still don't want to buzz me in. When I'm driving my $60,000 sports car, police suspect that I'm a drug dealer."

"I believe Julian and I have had a positive influence on our family and friends. Certainly my immediate family has had a change of consciousness. Individuals can change things on an individual level, but it's just a drop in the sea."

> "This country is very confused on a lot of issues. Look at the way we're totally sex obsessed and puritanical at the same time. I guess it's not surprising that we preach equal rights at the same time we inhabit a society with glass ceilings that prohibit equal opportunity."

"There's no doubt that your parents were raised to be much more racist than say, your nephews..."

"...who don't have a racist bone in their bodies..."

"Not that I can see. But nevertheless, even though there's clearly more respect and understanding between blacks and whites in the last few generations, as a 6'4" black man, I can't help but notice that not all whites are comfortable in my company. It seems to me that this country has embarked down a divisive road, where individuals invest an enormous amount of energy in their cultural heritage, whether it's kissing the blarney stone or celebrating Kwanzaa. Pride in one's ethnicity is fine, as long as it doesn't splinter the country into isolated groups. We shouldn't underestimate the rich multi-cultural diversity of being American. Having lived in Europe for years, it was interesting to see America through their eyes. It was also the only time in my life where I was perceived as simply an American, instead of a black American, like I am here. If you're a politician or a minister, maybe this is O.K., but if you're just a regular working guy it gets to be a drag. Always—spoken, or unspoken—there's this color deal. And it's really nice to go someplace where there's no color deal."

"Well, this country is very confused on a lot of issues," says Beverly. "Look at the way we're totally sex obsessed and puritanical at the same time. I guess it's not surprising that we preach equal rights at the same time we inhabit a society with glass ceilings that prohibit equal opportunity. We might espouse integration, but as an interracial couple, we're certainly aware of stares and double takes when we're out in public. When we see another interracial couple, we'll nudge each other and say, 'IRC, incoming at 2:00!'"

"We're still a rarity, but that too is slowly but surely changing. Life might be change, but when you're the one who has a lot invested in the change, it sure seems slow. We are still inherently a racist country, and the only way to breach the separation between blacks and whites is to acknowledge that the division exists and work from there. You certainly can't fix a problem if you don't admit you have one. And believe me, this country has a problem. I might have a law degree and a country club membership, but I'm still immediately judged by the color of my skin before anything else."

"Now here's something that I've never told anyone before, but when I came to my new job—and I could die for saying this—I came to my boss and told him, confessed, really, that I was married to a black man."

"Well, well, this is interesting...," chuckles Julian.

"I was too ashamed to ever mention it before. My boss blinked, caught his breath, and said, 'Thank you for telling me. It doesn't make any difference.' What terrible forces drive us to apologize for things we have no reason to apologize for?"

"What keeps me going," concludes Julian, "is my faith. I believe we are all children of God, and that it will be God's influence in our lives that will move us ahead."

Tanya and I share what I call a suburban American culture that gives us a lot in common. With a common culture, it makes our race seem irrelevant, or at least unimportant."

"My mom was more concerned over Gunnar's archeology degree being able to support a family than his race. Like many African American families, we know we have white blood in our veins. Both sides of my family are descendants of the slave/master relationship. Some relatives were so light skinned that they passed over to the white community."

"I was all too aware of our different races and was more than a little nervous how people, especially my family, would react. My parents were concerned that we would be rejected by the world around us if we stayed together, but frankly, they've been the only ones who have been clearly bothered by our relationship."

"When I first started my job providing business assistance to aspiring and existing entrepreneurs in the area, I was warned that some folks would have the assumption that a black woman couldn't possibly be helpful in business matters. They might start with that attitude, but I have the pleasure of changing their assumptions, because I do help them quite a bit. You can almost see this 'Wow!' happen, right in the middle of our consultation."

"If you think about it, you punish yourself most of all with your own prejudice. When parents try to make kids choose between them and the person they're in love with, parents often just end up losing that child. My dad threatened to disown me, but my mom was able to keep his anger from coming to that. He had this fantasy of a blond haired, blue-eyed grandchild, and it was really hard for him to let go of that dream."

"I had an interesting conversation with my father-in-law before Gunnar and I got married. I told him that when I told my mother that I was marrying his son, her concern was not the color of his skin, but whether he was ambitious enough to be my professional equal. I said if I wanted to be a snob, I could accuse his entire family of not being equal to mine, because we're all better educated, with good professions, therefore he has no right not to accept me, because in every way I'm a worthy mate for his son. He said he couldn't argue with me. In fact, his own pastor had urged him to 'get over it', but he was still struggling."

"When Tanya got pregnant, Dad wasn't nearly as excited as I'd hoped he'd be, yet once he held Genesis and spent some time with her, you could see a twinkle in his eye. In my parents' defense, all people have some form of prejudice. It's human nature to categorize and label, group and stereotype. It's a challenge for everyone to look beyond our expectations and assumptions and accept each person on his or her own merits. It's quite possible that when Genesis has boyfriends, her choice in romantic partner might not necessarily be someone I would have picked out for her.

"What's fascinating is that most people don't think of themselves as racist, and can quite easily accept black and white mixing among their children's classmates or co-workers. Being friends is one thing, but dating and marriage—forget it! That's the line that a lot of people can't cross."

At the same time, I feel uncomfortable making any excuses for racism, because it's inexcusably wrong."

"What's fascinating is that most people don't think of themselves as racist, and can quite easily accept black and white mixing among their children's classmates or co-workers. Being friends is one thing, but dating and marriage—forget it! That's the line that a lot of people can't cross."

1 was shocked when he asked me to the prom, but really glad he did—even though I wasn't allowed to go."

"But we started talking on the phone after that and by the spring before graduation, she was my girlfriend. My parents started being concerned that I wasn't spending enough time with people of my own race. My school and ball teams were mostly white, and now so was my first real girlfriend. They sent me to an all-black college, so for the first time in my life I wasn't a minority. The students there certainly didn't approve of me dating Melissa, and it wasn't just because she was still in high school. They used to call me O.J. and I can't say I took that as a compliment. My best friend, who was white, went to Catawba College and loved it, so that's how I got interested in transferring here."

"My aunt and uncle had known R.J. for years, because he was on their son's ball team, so they knew he was a really good person. They loved him playing ball with my cousins, but weren't so enthusiastic about us dating. At first, my dad didn't seem to mind, but as time went by and he began to realize that we were in love, he didn't approve. At least my mom has come around. After five years, she respects how serious we are about each other."

"It's been really tough for me and my family. They definitely didn't approve of me dating outside my race and I hated feeling like they were trying to make me choose between them and Melissa. My dad and stepmother have really had a hard time with it. My real mom has been more understanding."

"For years, it was a struggle for us to be together as a couple, but now that we're both here at college together, we feel like we're finally someplace where people can just accept us as fellow students. The place feels like a family that really gives you support. I felt isolated all through high school, but since coming here last year, I feel surrounded by friends."

"My faith in Jesus has always given me strength. I just don't know how people can call themselves Christians and still be racist. You just know that the color of a person's skin is of no concern to Him," says R.J.

"We were both raised up as Southern Baptists, but his was the black church and mine was the white church. It's funny, if you think about it, because I don't think heaven is segregated!"

"My dad is like a different person now. He hugs me and tells me he loves me. When he calls on the phone, he always asks how Melissa is doing. It's as if for years they tried to keep us apart by withholding their love. But after so many years of us continuing to stand side-by-side, my dad, like Melissa's mom, has come to accept us as the real thing."

"It's still uncomfortable for me when I'm visiting his home, because I feel left out and can't keep up."

"She just sits there quietly, with her hands folded, and my family doesn't know quite what to make of her. It frustrates me, because they can't see how much fun she is." R.J. turns to Melissa and says, "It's like you're

> "We were both raised up as Southern Baptists, but his was the black church and mine was the white church. It's funny, if you think about it, because I don't think heaven is segregated!"

hiding yourself."

"His family is always picking and joking, and I know that's the way they show affection, but sometimes it makes me feel insecure."

"Well, sitting there so quiet probably makes them feel you don't like them!"

"What's really amazing to me," says Melissa quietly, "is after five years together, this is the first time we've ever talked about these things. As much as we want to do the right thing, it's so easy to misunderstand or be misunderstood. I'm not saying that prejudice doesn't exist, because I know it does, but a lot of things that we think are hostility or disrespect are just misunderstandings."

B ecause blacks so often have to deal with discrimination, it can make you more sensitive than someone who always expects to get their way. I've had cashiers refuse a local check because of insufficient ID, then turn right to the next (white) customer, and accept her out-of-state check, with even less ID! It certainly never occurs to Steve that someone won't take his check. I had a white friend in school who told me she and her friends could shoplift anything they wanted, because security was always following the black customers. It's like the white kids are innocent until proven guilty and the black kids are guilty until proven innocent."

"We've talked about our kids' racial identity when they get older,"says Steve. "Adam's a little darker than Joshua, so he might have no choice [but to identify with being black], but it's a sorry shame that we live in a society where everyone has to take a racial stand."

"Black culture has always assumed that if one of your parents is black, then you're black. The rest of society is going to treat you that way, so you might as well accept it. Of course, most black people are different shades of brown, and most whites are shades of pink and beige—so all of this labeling is silly anyway. When I hear the term 'colored people,' I think of the worst kind of segregation. Yet when I hear African American, I don't really relate to Africa. Identity and ethnic pride are fine, but forcing people to have a label is not."

"In the meanwhile, everything's so complicated," sighs Steve. "I've had black friends who won't take their white girlfriends home to meet their mother, because she'll get on them and say, 'What – I'm not good enough for you?'"

"It seems like anything pertaining to race always makes people jump to conclusions. When I worked for IBM, my black girlfriends would ask me, 'So, you don't like black men? Was your father a bad man? Did he walk out on your family?' I'm like, 'When did I say that, and what does that have to do with my feelings for Steve? My father's black, and I love him. He's a good man, and my love for my husband is in no way a bad reflection on my father.'"

"Even though I married into a black family, and know all of their stories, I wouldn't presume to know firsthand what it's like to be black in this country. I got so angry during the vice-presidential debates when the candidates were asked what they'd do if they were black and were pulled over for DWB (driving while black)."

Kathy bursts into laughter and says, "There's no way those two [Cheney and Lieberman] could answer that question!"

"The only way to answer that question is to say, 'Are you an idiot? How in the world could I possibly tell you what it's like to be a black person in America? I haven't ever had to deal with the racist assumptions that follow black Americans everywhere. If I did, I'm sure I'd be a different person.' What's important about getting stories of black American reality out to White America is it helps change subconscious behavior."

"I remember," continues Kathy, "Oprah Winfrey did a show where

> "When I hear the term 'colored people', I think of the worst kind of segregation. Yet when I hear African American, I don't really relate to Africa. Identity and ethnic pride are fine, but forcing people to have a label is not."

she darkened a white man's skin and lightened a black man's skin, and had them both dressed in the same clothes. Then she sent them both out on to the sidewalk to ask passersby for the time. As soon as the darker man spoke to someone, they sped up and hurried away. But when the light skin man spoke to a stranger, they'd stop right away and say, 'What can I do for you?' That TV audience was stunned into silence. The separate experiences were so apparent, there was no room for coincidence."

"As a family, race has not been an issue," says Steve. "But as a nation, as far as race relations are concerned, we've still got a long way to go."

JENNIFER MATHIS & DONNELL HOPKINS

"We met at a bar two years ago, and we've been together ever since," says twenty-three-year-old Jennifer. "We've basically lived together since the first night we met."

"When that song 'Doin' Da Butt' came on, I got so carried away dancing with her that I ripped my pants right down the middle. I just untucked my shirt and kept on going—I sure wasn't going to leave her on the dance floor without me."

"Growing up in Lubbock, Texas, I knew that interracial dating wasn't accepted there, but I was never taught racist values at home. My mom always raised me to believe that everyone is equal, but when I started dating a black guy, all of a sudden she became totally disapproving. I had stepped over an invisible line that I didn't know was there. I judge people completely on their character instead of their color. Two years of us being together only makes her more upset than ever. I guess she was hoping he was only a phase! My dad doesn't even know we're together. I love the closeness and unconditional love in Donnell's family."

"My own family has always practiced what they preached. Jennifer has been totally accepted by my mom and my grandma. The way we look at it, everyone puts their shoes on just the same. You step in one pant leg, and then the other. We all live, then we all die, so why should our pigment make that much difference? One thing I have noticed, going out with a white girl, is that most racists are cowards. They make comments under their breath, behind your back. Maybe they're ashamed. They should be."

"I feel the most disapproval from black girls," confides Jennifer. "When we're out at a club, they'll bump into me real hard, trying to pick a fight, but I won't take the bait. My black girlfriend says their anger at a black man with a white woman is because so many eligible black guys are either dead or in jail. Look at the O.J. Simpson verdict. It hurts me that those black women on the jury didn't seem to care that Nicole was brutally murdered. They just didn't want another black man convicted. I can understand it, but it still saddens me. Johnnie Cochran just threw gas on the fires of racial tension. That trial was the one thing Donnell and I would argue over."

"The black community has a different relationship towards the police than whites. It's not so difficult for us to believe that the glove was planted and that blood evidence was tampered with because we all know people who were framed and harassed by the police. I've never been in any trouble with the police, but I realize that when people see me coming they might sense danger, because so many black males are either in jail or on parole. It's totally unfair, yet that's the way it is. Both of us work two jobs to pay the bills and don't bother anyone, but we know that not everyone wishes us well."

"Our goals are pretty simple," says Jennifer. "We want to stay out of debt and raise a family. I don't really understand why that should bother

> "One thing I have noticed, going out with a white girl, is that most racists are cowards. They make comments under their breath, behind your back. Maybe they're ashamed. They should be."

anyone, but the way my mom reacts, you'd think we were doing something terrible."

"My mom is just the opposite. She'd love for us to make her a grandmother. Unlike a lot of my generation, I don't think life is a game. I'm not interested in fast cars and making a fast buck. I want to build up something that lasts."

"I think all the MTV and rap videos give kids the wrong idea of what life's all about. It's all so materialistic and can really give you hollow values. Flashy stuff doesn't feed your heart. I used to be all swept up in all the cool status symbols that I'd see on TV before I fell in love with Donnell."

Both of my parents have a Caribbean background, and I grew up in a racially mixed town in New Jersey," says Melanie. "When I came out at nineteen, even though my parents had gay friends, it was difficult at first to accept it in their daughter. Catherine and I have been together as a couple for nine years now, and they really know her and love her. They accept us as a family."

"When you love someone and that person goes down an unexpected path, that's an opportunity for growth and change," Catherine adds. "That's the push for people to be 'out' in the lesbian, gay or bisexual community, because when people discover that someone they love and respect is gay, they often become more accepting, more tolerant, and even celebratory. The same holds true for interracial families. When a child gets together with someone of a different race, the parents get to know that 'in-law' as an individual and see beyond their stereotypes and prejudice. My family didn't let me down when I got involved with Melanie. My parents (one Jewish and the other Episcopalian) had always been supportive of individuality and personal freedom. I was the first in the family to have a significant relationship with someone of a different race, so that was an opportunity for them to experience something new."

"We're really very lucky to have the family support that we enjoy from both sides. We've known lots of couples whose families are not able to respect either their racial or sexual variance from what was expected of them. When people see us as a couple–with our three kids, our family–it's not like anything you see on TV."

"Both Melanie and I always knew we wanted to be mothers, and had lesbian friends who were mothers, so it was only a question of how and when. Mel got pregnant first. She gave birth to Sadie, and I gave birth to Kofi and Rio."

"We consciously decided to have biracial kids. It just makes sense to us."

"After all," continues Catherine, "we are an interracial couple. If we were a straight couple, we wouldn't have a choice about our biological kids. They would be biracial."

"Both of the men who donated their sperm are friends of ours and wanted to help us create a family. We went through the legal process of having Catherine adopt Sadie and me adopt Kofi and Rio, so now we're the two legal parents of all our kids."

"Sadie calls me 'Mommy' and Melanie 'Mama', but she uses 'Mom' for both of us. Mel went back to work a couple of months after she gave birth to Sadie, and I stayed home with her in the day for two years. When I was out with Sadie, there was this assumption that I had a black husband. I was stumped when people would ask, 'Is her father black?' After I gave birth to Kofi and Rio, Mel stopped working outside of the house and stays home with the kids during the day."

> "When a child gets together with someone of a different race, the parents get to know that 'in-law' as an individual and see beyond their stereotypes and prejudice."

"People would say to me, 'Wow! You look so good for having just had twins,' laughs Melanie, "and I'd just smile and say 'Thank-you.' Over the years we've lost the compulsion to explain our life story to people who ask casual questions. It's not that we're secretive, because there's no shame in how our family came to be. I do believe that the more people understand about the truth of things, how they really are, the less threatening our differences become and the more apparent our similarities become."

"The fact that we're artists and activists who've chosen to live in New York City gives us an incredibly diverse circle of friends. Our kids will grow

up knowing a variety of different family groups and assuming they're all equally important . The more you're exposed to differences, the more natural, comfortable, and exciting it feels to live in this big world."

"The culture, at large, is unfortunately not always as accepting as our friends and family. Trying to find children's books that don't make racial and sexual stereotypes can be hard. For example, in *Madeline's Rescue*, when the little girls find a dog and want to keep it, they're met with 'I dare say, said Lord Cuckoo Face, I mean it's a perfect disgrace, for young ladies to embrace this creature of uncertain race.' We changed the words to 'uncertain place'."

"We change the words in the kids books all the time," continues Catherine. "You have to if you want your kids' stories to help them identify with the culture of their neighborhood and family. One thing that's different about our family is that our kids have two parents who both have an equal impact and involvement in their lives. We're both around, physically and emotionally. We both make their lunches. We both read to them and take them to the doctor. They're lucky for all of that and so are we."

"We consciously decided to have biracial kids. It makes sense to us. After all, we are an interracial couple. If we were a straight couple, we wouldn't have a choice about our biological kids. They would be biracial."

Keith starts right in with his family history, obviously having given it thought before now. "My mother and father were both drug and alcohol addicts. My father wasn't around much but eventually my mom got sober and became a Christian. In the meanwhile, I was not a very moral individual during my early teenage years. Growing up in inner city Chicago, there were a lot of things to get involved in, most of which were not good. You could say I was rebellious, but I really didn't have any rules to rebel against. I played football from third grade through high school, and that's probably what kept me in school. Football got me through high school, but it was the Lord that brought me to college. After I was saved, my pastors thought I should go to Bible college."

"We have totally opposite backgrounds," offers LeeAnn. "I grew up in the small rural town of Owosso, Michigan. My parents were conservative churchgoers, so I had plenty of rules to break–and I did! My boyfriend and I got involved with drugs and alcohol. I even ran away from home for a little while. I missed a lot of school, but was able to catch up and graduate on time. I met Keith at Bible college, which was our common ground."

"I had made a promise to the Lord that I wouldn't date for one year. I had been so promiscuous before I was saved, that I knew I needed some time to get a new perspective on women. LeeAnn was the first girl I had a friendship with, instead of just trying to make time. Growing up, it had never occurred to me that I would marry outside of my race. I denied the fact that I was falling for her."

"The same with me, as far as dating outside of my own race. It didn't at first occur to me to look at Keith as anything other than a friend. I was also like Keith in that I'd been through enough mess dating, that I was through with fooling around. I wasn't even interested in dating someone unless I could imagine marrying them. So when someone first mentioned to me that they thought Keith was romantically interested in me, it was unimaginable. But the idea stuck with me, and after a few weeks of thinking about us as a couple, it didn't seem so unimaginable anymore. I approached him one day in the school cafeteria and said, 'I'm attracted to you and think we should start dating.'"

"I felt the same way, but was concerned that it might affect our effectiveness in church ministry, so we spoke to the college president about our concerns of being a couple and he said that there was nothing in the Bible that should dissuade us. The interesting thing to me is the very strong similarities between LeeAnn and my mom. They struggled with all sorts of mess, but they both found the Lord and are now good Christian women. There are no two women in this world that I admire more. I'd grown up hearing my mom saying, 'I'm tired of black men going with white women,' so I was more than a little anxious to tell her about my growing feelings for LeeAnn. After the first time they met, she told me she knew LeeAnn was going to be my wife and that we had her blessing. My grandfather, being from a much older generation, had a real hard

> "My grandfather's change of heart towards her softened his feelings for the entire white race, I think. He's in his eighties now, and he loves to say how it took a twenty-year-old girl from Owosso, Michigan, to open his eyes and change his mind."

time with the idea of me with a white woman–at least until he met her. From that day forward, he refers to her as 'my girl'. He's just crazy about her. My grandfather's change of heart towards her softened his feelings for the entire white race, I think. He's in his eighties, and loves to say how it took a twenty-year-old girl from Owosso, Michigan to open his eyes and change his mind."

"Two years later, we were engaged to be married and had the blessing of both our families. I lived with his grandmother in Chicago the year before we married. She was like the grandmother to the entire

neighborhood and there was a steady stream of people through her apartment. It was hard on me because I just wasn't used to it. Life in the inner city is like another country. We had a big wedding in my hometown, even Keith's father was there. The dean of students and his wife were in the wedding party. We had soul food at the rehearsal dinner…"

"And there were some guests there that had never had a fried chicken wing," laughs Keith. "Seriously, though, the wedding vows are a wonderful way to spread the word of God."

"Now we're both ordained as youth ministers. Keith works full time as a youth minister and I work as a receptionist at the church here in Durham (NC). I was nervous moving to the South as an interracial couple, because of the things I'd seen in the movies."

"The surprise for both of us when we got here was that we've been stared at a lot less since we moved here. Maybe it's because there are so many colleges around this area that people are more open-minded, but I

"To me, some of the most beautiful children are interracial children, and that just speaks volumes. The kids are as lovely as anything in God's creation. It proves to me that the races were meant to be together and not segregated. Unless all the races are united together, we'll never live up to our fullest human potential."

swear we felt a lot more disapproval in Chicago than we do here."

"Especially with older couples and black women, you could just feel the anger in their stare. I'm sensitive to their point of view, but it's their point of view, not mine."

"Black women in the inner city just hate to see their men go off to get an education and come back from college with a white woman on their arm. They see it as a betrayal, but there's no doubt in my mind that LeeAnn and I are meant to be together."

"The black teenage girls that I council at church, will say to me, 'Miss LeeAnn, you're not white,' and I'll laugh and say 'I'm as white as anyone around.' I think they're surprised to realize that a white person can be likable, which shows you how much distrust is still between the races. Fear of the unknown can only dissolve by getting to know each other."

"Funnily enough, being married to LeeAnn has given me a whole new appreciation of my African American culture—the language, the food, the music—the whole pace of the community—is something that I've experienced again through her eyes. She would always question things I just took for granted."

"For example, I could never understand how any mention of 'your mama' could start a fight, but I've come to appreciate the importance, the place of respect, that older black women have in African American culture."

"Our goal as parents is to have our daughter go visit my family back in Chicago, so she can experience the good parts of the African American community, and not just be scared off by the things you see on TV or read in the paper. My people might live in tight quarters and not have a lot of money to spend, but they somehow manage to keep a smile on their face, while I look at the folks in the upper echelons, and they don't even look like they're having a good time! I don't want her looking up or down at anyone because of their possessions. I want my daughter to know about soul food, not through a marketing strategy at Kroger's, but on her own family table."

"When I go back to my little hometown, it seems like a place where no one ever changes. I guess it's because they never left. Living in different parts of the country, with people of different backgrounds has changed me—I think for the better."

"One thing we try to do in our youth ministry, which is predominately black, is teach the kids not to be so ethnocentric. We want to encourage the kids not to ghettoize themselves with slang, to broaden their world with expanded language. We show them a world outside of rap music and sports. The saddest thing about poor, black communities is there are so few role models—especially for the boys. The few young men who do make something of themselves tend to move out of the neighborhood and never

look back. It's my calling to show boys how to be decent men. I want to say respect where you came from, but make a plan for a better tomorrow. Teenagers can look at the family that LeeAnn and I have created as a bridge between the black and white community. We don't reject one side or the other. The street goes both ways. We'll raise our own child the same way, with an appreciation for the worthwhile traditions in both black and white cultures."

"To me, some of the most beautiful children are interracial children, and that just speaks volumes. God created us, black and white, and when you look at the product of interracial unions, whether it's Asian and white, or black and Latino—whatever the mix—the kids are as lovely as anything in God's creation. It proves to me that the races were meant to be together and not segregated. Unless all the races are united together, we'll never live up to our fullest human potential. Every race and culture could benefit from the lessons of each other. Fear and ignorance keep us apart, and that is not the will of God.

As a girl, when I discovered that both of my parents were part Native American, I got really interested in that culture and started doing a lot of research on my own. I always felt different from my half sisters, with their red hair and blue eyes, and my blond-haired, blue-eyed half brother. I probably used my heritage as a retreat from feeling like an outsider in my own family. My own mom was extremely racist towards African Americans, which I could never understand or accept. Growing up, the kids at school would look at me and ask, 'What are you?' I was neither light or dark enough. When I made black friends, my mom would say, 'Why don't you stick with your own kind?' and I'd say, 'Exactly what is my kind, Mom?' Mexican, Asian, Jewish, would have been fine with her. But black—forget it!"

"My sister and Dottie were friends from school and we met when I was eighteen, while she was working at the truck stop restaurant. I was raised not to be worried about someone's color. There's good and bad in all colors. I've always had white friends and black friends all my life. In the countryside, it seems like it's always been that way."

"My mom moved out-of-state, and that's been sort of a blessing, because frankly, she was a problem. We didn't need to hear her running around calling me a nigger lover. She wouldn't even allow my siblings to speak to me when John and I first got together."

"If she walked in that door right now" says John, "I'd have to find somewhere to go."

"Better leave the room than say or do something. There's not a thing John can do to change my mom's mind. The man holds down four different jobs and has always been good to me and the kids, but a racist can't see anything as important besides their own hate. As a parent, the worst thing is to see racial hatred aimed at your kids. My son was invited to a friend's house to go swimming with kids from school, and when the girl's dad drives up and sees Doug in the pool with his classmates, he pulls out a gun and starts screaming, 'Mother fucking niggers! That's what's wrong with America today—a white man can't have anything today because of niggers.

Get your black ass out of my pool and get the fuck off my property!'"

"This was one time I couldn't just lay back and do nothing," John quietly goes on, "but at the same time, I didn't want to sink to his level, because I was raised to understand that two wrongs don't make a right. I went to his store and asked him if he had a daughter. Then I asked him what would he do if she came home and told him that someone put a gun on her. He said 'I'd probably pull one myself.' I said 'That's what I feel like doing when you pull a gun on my son,'—then I walked on out the store. He just stood there, frozen, without moving."

"Our daughter, who looks white, has friends from school who aren't allowed to come to her home because she's from a mixed family. Some of her friends aren't even allowed to receive a phone call from a black classmate! The crazy thing is these kids are all in school together, doing

> "I long for the day when you don't have to declare your race. At least now, like on my son's college applications, you can check two race boxes. It's the first time we've acknowledged that you can be both African American and white at the same time."

sports and cheerleading together, and those parents that won't let their kids even talk on the phone with blacks are up in the bleachers cheering the black kids on. They let their kids go to the school dances, yet they won't let them get a phone call. Their attitude is 'You don't cross my threshold. As long as you stay outside of my house, we're fine.'"

"I believe if you have that kind of race hatred in you, you'll always have it in you. I don't think it goes away until it dies with you. That's why I don't spend a whole lot of time trying to change people's minds about things."

I met my husband's aunt at a hospital where I worked as a nurse's aid. She invited me to her home and I started talking to Jesus, and we've been talking ever since," says Robin, in the living room of their newly built and furnished house. Even with two young children, there's not a speck on the wall and the upholstered sofa is showroom fresh.

"I was still learning the English, and Robin tried to speak the Spanish with me, which I really appreciated. I'd grown up in Mexico, and was still not so good in English. When we met, I didn't pay her color any mind. Mexicans come in all colors, so I don't even notice that stuff much. I just saw that she was a nice girl who was making an effort to speak to me."

"It seems like a lot of white folks raise their kids to not be prejudiced, but if their children start dating outside their race—forget it! Friendships from school, work or sports—fine—but don't integrate the family! I grew up with a lot of white best girlfriends and I was always welcome in their home, as long as I didn't date their brother. My own family raised me to be concerned about a person's character, not their race. That didn't change when I started dating Jessie. What I really liked about him the first time we met was I could tell he was a serious person, someone who wanted to build a good life for himself. He wasn't afraid of hard work, and that made me interested in him, because I don't have any use for someone who won't pull their own weight."

"I never had much problem finding work. I used to do orchard work, and now I lay pipe for construction. There's always plenty of work to be done, and I'm not afraid of it."

"A woman needs a man who will take care of his family. That's much more important than the color of his skin. I know some families go all to pieces when a family member marries outside their race, but they usually soften when the kids are born. An innocent little baby can soften the hardest heart. Both of our kids look more Mexican than African American, so I sometimes get a few stares when I'm out with them. It seems like in general, white people are much more concerned about race mixing. Which is pretty funny when you realize that back in the days of

slavery, white babies were raised by black wet nurses! Black folk have always known what goes on. If you think about it, very few black Americans are pure African. My mom is real light, whereas my dad is dark. Most black families have people of all colors."

Growing up in Mexico, I could never imagine that life would be so good. Here a man can take much better care of his family. There's enough work to save and build up something of value. You can never really know what this life is going to bring, it's shorter than you think, so you got to try and do your best, because this is the only chance you get."

"The Latino and black cultures are a good mix. Whenever they have a party, they always bring their kids. In California, you see a lot of that mix. I think Hispanics are a lot less racist than whites. Some white folks will

> "It seems like in general, white people are more concerned about race mixing. Which is pretty funny when you realize that back in the days of slavery, white babies had black wet nurses!"

look right through you in a way that Latinos never do. Especially the rich ones. You can tell they feel superior. I don't let it bother me, because I feel like that's more their problem than mine. When I meet people, it's almost like I can read their eyes. Like when I met my husband, I could tell right away that he was a good man."

"If someone judges me because I don't speak so good English, I don't let it bother me, because they don't pay my bills!"

"It's so important for people to understand other people's experiences and for people to understand that our marriage isn't about our race. It's about our love and respect for each other. Love is the same in all colors."

My sister got her face all frowned up when she found out we were getting married, which is kind of silly, since our own grandmother looked as white as can be. My mother and her sister both are bright white—a lot of my relatives are downright pale, so I can hardly see why my sister would disapprove of Jackie's race. I don't mean no harm, but I don't need to spend my entire paycheck on a ninety dollar hairdo and foot-long fingernails! I'd always been involved with black women before I was with Jackie and they loved to spend my money in a way Jackie never has. When I see these black women all decked out like an African Queen, I think to myself, 'Woman, you ain't from nowhere near Africa! You know you're from right around the corner.' Put that sister out there in Africa and she'd have no idea what to do."

"If anything," Jackie remarks, "I think that the black community is in some ways less accepting of interracial relationships nowadays than whites are—especially the African American women. If a black guy gets with a white woman, especially if he marries her, they don't like it one bit! I'm really aware of their resentment sometimes."

"Race mixing has been going on forever," says Sam. "Look at Sally Hemings and Thomas Jefferson. You couldn't stop it then, and there's no stopping it today, because love and sex are a fact of life. In this day and age all people should be free to be with who they want to be with. A whole lot of people fought and died for me to have that right and I'm not going to give that up."

"When my mom first found out I was with a black man, she says 'I didn't raise you to be with niggers,'" remembers Jackie, with a shudder. "I had never heard her say a racist thing before, so I was completely surprised by her attitude. Like a lot of people, she's O.K. with any race, as long as you don't bring them inside the family. Heck, if you don't invite folks in the front door, they'll just be sneaking in through the window, so there's no sense in trying to stop the unstoppable. Segregation is over, and

I say good riddance."

"I don't go for things like the Million Man March. It doesn't do the country any good to separate black and white. Black power, Ku Klux Klan—they're both about building up one race at the cost of another."

"Yeah," adds Jackie, "all that stuff about keeping the race 'pure' sounds like a laundry detergent ad. What does it have to do with the human heart? Love is not a color. Look at our kids—people come in all colors—and have for a long time. That's why so many white folks have had such a hard time accepting that Thomas Jefferson was making those babies with Sally Hemings. It's like they're afraid that accepting that truth will make it O.K. for everyone else. It's nothing the black community hasn't known all along."

> "All that stuff about keeping the race 'pure' sounds like a laundry detergent ad. What does it have to do with the human heart? Love is not a color."

Laughing, Sam joins in, "Those white folks have lots of crazy ways of looking at things. Look at President Clinton. I say, if the man is going to get some booty, leave him alone. It ain't anyone's business, except maybe his wife's. It's certainly no reason to tear the country apart! Seems like people are scared to death about sex. It's just a fact of life."

"Think of the term 'nigger lover'—a phrase I'm all too familiar with. As if you're supposed to dislike your own race if you care for someone of another race. People try to use the Bible to keep the races apart, but there's references to race mixing all over the place back in the Biblical days. One bumper sticker I'd put on my car is, 'I'm a member of the human race.'"

had never dated anyone outside of the black community before I started going out with Derwood, though as the second black nurse ever hired at the hospital, I was certainly comfortable around white people. Growing up, my dad was a barber for white men and my best friend in grade school was a white doctor's daughter, which was really unusual for that day and time. My parents died when I was young, but my older sister, who had taken on that role, was very displeased about my relationship with Derwood. We were estranged for years as a result. We've rebuilt a good relationship over the years, but it was painful there for a while."

"I remember when we decided to get married and a friend said, 'You'll probably have to resign from the country club,' and I said, 'Like hell! They'll have to throw me out!' which they never did."

"I was probably the first black member there, through my marriage to Derwood, and I certainly remember my initial discomfort of walking into that dining room and being stared at. The members at that time weren't used to seeing a black woman there unless she had a tray in her hand."

"You've got to remember, that back then there were still quite a few private clubs that didn't admit women or blacks. Of course, that's all changed now in the past twenty years. It seems slow sometimes, especially if you're the one doing the changes. Today, no one gives Johanna a second glance in the club dining room and my sister and Johanna are good friends. But twenty some years ago when we drove down to Alabama to see her, she didn't want us driving into her driveway, for fear of her neighbors' reactions."

"People change, things change, but just because you want something to be some way, it doesn't make it so," muses Johanna. "I'm not going to dwell on a slight, but for some reason, I think I'm more aware of people's disapproval now than when I was younger. Maybe it's the obliviousness of youth that has worn away over the years, but I'm more aware of subtle digs."

"We share the same conservative values, which helps us see eye-to-eye, not only on the big picture, but also on most daily issues. The liberal press and democrats would have you believe that conservative republicans are all secret,

if not overt, racists, which obviously is pretty absurd. I was the first president of Junior Achievement when the schools were segregated, and we recruited kids out of the black and white high schools and integrated our academic teams years before the schools did. I always thought the segregation of restaurants was so goddamned stupid. Black women could come in and try on brassieres at the department store, but they couldn't sit down at the lunch counter and have a cup of coffee. I never could see the logic in that!"

"The local schools were desegregated the year after I graduated and there was a lot of racial tension in town. My dad lost some of his clients at the barbershop as a result. On the whole, the black community was very reluctant to get actively involved in the Civil Rights Movement. They cherished their middle class status and didn't want to do anything to upset the apple cart. Of

> "I remember when we decided to get married, and a friend said 'You'll probably have to resign from the country club,'" says Derwood. Johanna laughs as she adds, "The members at that time weren't used to seeing a black woman there unless she had a tray in her hand."

course, there's a lot an individual can do to promote understanding without marching in the street. I've been putting together for the school systems a program of Negro spirituals in concert form, along with a lecture series, which has been very rewarding and worthwhile. I sing with the Opera Society, which brings me great joy. I take pleasure in all types of music."

"I can't imagine any white woman having any finer qualities than Johanna. Her sense of humor, consideration, and common sense are even more important to me than her beauty as the years go by. She's been my best friend for a long time."

Sharon begins, "I'm from a large Irish Catholic family in northern Virginia. My childhood was totally segregated except for black maids."

"My father was a diplomat in Ethiopia," says her husband, Yitna, "so we did a lot of traveling around and I was always exposed to different races. In 1970, it was almost as if the entire youth of Ethiopia was waiting in line to come to America. I came when I was sixteen, with a student visa, and finished high school in northern Virginia. I met Sharon at college. She and I were part of a group of students interested in poetry and writing."

"When Yitna and I started becoming a couple, I guess I just assumed that he was not the picture of the son-in-law my parents had imagined for me. But when you are young and in love, you feel like you can take on the world. We were beneficiaries of the Civil Rights Movement. We never felt the slightest bit apologetic for our feelings toward each other."

"I've never really felt much racism against myself. They called us "kushi" and "mavro" when we lived in Israel and Greece, sometimes derogatorily, sometimes with fascination. My color was not reflected back at me the same way it would have been had I grown up in the U.S."

"The fascinating and confusing thing about the legacy of slave culture in America," muses Sharon, "is that blacks and whites were living side by side at the same time they were segregated from each other. Look at Thomas Jefferson and Sally Hemings. Their relationship is a perfect example of the confusion over miscegenation in this country. What an ugly word! It sounds so judgmental and condemning. The Clarence Thomas hearings are another example of rampant racial stereotyping. He's still a lightning rod for racial politics."

"It's mythic, really, the powerful imagery of light and dark, good and evil. Fear."

"The demonization of blackness can be powerful stuff," continues Sharon. "Look at the Willie Horton political ads of the Bush [Sr.] campaign. The TV screen was filled with the glowering face of this dark skinned black man. It became an eighties icon of race hate. It tapped into White America's latent racism. The middle class fears the seething black underclass in the same way the slave owner feared the slave."

"The color of one's skin is really an endless obsession. Think of all the terms that are used to describe skin color—cocoa, dusky, café au lait, high yellow."

"I think of our family as being part of the beige revolution," laughs Sharon. "Segregation happens in countless ways, whether it's the Hatfields and the McCoys, the caste system in India or Jim Crow in the South. I look at our kids as the ultimate act of integration and the hope for the world's races being truly integrated in the future. The power of Martin Luther King was his vision for racial harmony based on the spiritual and not the political. His adaptation of Gandhi's philosophy of nonviolence was a very holistic approach and transcended our impulse to see discreet groups, embracing the totality of all humanity. In mathematics, you first learn differentiation

> "Segregation always creates inequality, because it promotes the fear of the other, the unknown. Mixed children make segregation impossible and permanently break down the color line.

and then you learn integration. It's a more evolved concept."

"The argument 'What about the children?' is an interesting one," offers Yitna. "It's as if folks fear that interracial kids are somehow at a disadvantage because they didn't get to choose being biracial. Well, no one gets to choose their parents! Mixed kids blend the separatism of 'you people.' They make it difficult to hold people responsible for their race."

"A great American fallacy is 'separate but equal.' Segregation always creates inequality, because it promotes the fear of the other, the unknown. Mixed children make segregation impossible and permanently break down the color line."

1'd dated other white girls before, but Candy was the first one I brought home to my mother."

"I was concerned about my dad meeting Greg, because he was from the old school, where you didn't tolerate any racial mixing. Like Greg, I'd dated people of other races, but I never brought any of them home. But I knew from the start that Greg was it for me. I'd had Hodgkin's disease at sixteen and then I lost my mom, so I just felt like going for the good that I could find in life and not putting off what's important. I asked him to marry me two weeks after we met. We set the date for a few months later. But even after we got married, I'd take off my wedding ring every time I'd see my dad."

"Back in those times, if people didn't want to be bothered, you just left them alone. I honestly didn't worry too much about what her dad might or might not think about me because of my race. I just didn't let it be my problem. To tell the truth, I don't think he had any real problems with our marriage, except to worry about what his friends would say. Once we finally met, we got along fine. I've lived in the same area all my life, and I've seen a lot of changes in race relations. I went to segregated schools until the middle of high school. I think the fact that I played sports helped make me comfortable with the white kids. The kids who played team sports in school had a lot easier time adapting to integration. The neighborhoods weren't integrated and you certainly didn't see any biracial couples. It was against the law. Interracial dating was not accepted back then. If a black guy dated a white girl, we'd call him an 'Uncle Tom' and you know what they call a white person that dates a black...." Greg hesitates over the term, then says–"Nigger lover."

"Twenty-some years ago guys would call me that to try to get Greg to fight with them, but I'd talk him out of stepping into that trap. Early on, we'd get stares when we were out in public, but nowadays people don't pay us much mind. Greg's brother is married to a Swedish woman and my sister is dating a black man, so we've come a long way from having to hide my wedding ring from my father. I can honestly say that as far as Greg and I are concerned, race is not an issue between us."

"Our son Brandon is very light skinned, but he definitely considers himself black, even though he has a white girlfriend ," says Greg. "That's one of the good things about there being more racial equality–black folk are less likely to try and pass for white. They can be more proud of themselves. Brandon is totally comfortable around everyone. He's always had friends of all races–color doesn't make any difference to him."

"One thing I have noticed, is that Brandon's white girlfriends' parents don't accept him as easily as his black girlfriends' parents do. The black parents see him as a light-skinned black man and the white parents don't see the white part of him at all."

> "The older people are going to have to die off, because they are too set in their ways to ever change. It's going to be up to the younger people to continue what the Civil Rights Movement started. Kids like our son are the best hope for the future."

"One on one, people can get along pretty good, but in groups, people often can turn ugly. There's never been a time in history when some people didn't have hate in them. Sometimes I think race is only an excuse for those kind of people to hate. And I don't care how many books you write, the people who are prejudiced aren't going to change. The older people are going to have to die off, because they are too set in their ways to ever change. It's going to be up to the younger people to continue what the Civil Rights Movement started. Kids like our son are the best hope for the future."

My first association with anyone of color wasn't until I joined the Army, working along with a Japanese fellow for a black sergeant in Ft. Hood Texas."

"I grew up on a farm in South Carolina, and went to segregated schools. I joined the Reserves in 1979, and that's when I met Henry, and I'm glad I did. He was the sweetest, most caring man I'd ever met. I had never dated a white guy before. Never even thought about it. That was a 'no-no' where I come from, but he made me change my mind."

"Of course, at my age and background, I certainly had never dated across the color line either. My feelings for Veronica were so strong that I had to act on them, even though some of my family was terribly upset..."

"His sister wouldn't speak to him for years."

"I remember being at a funeral in Georgia after we'd been married for about five years. My brother didn't want to have anything to do with us either, but when he saw my aunts enjoying themselves so much sitting next to Veronica, he realized that she was a woman that he could enjoy. He's come to realize that my wife is just as crazy and fun as he is. You should have seen them dancing at his daughter's wedding. They cut a rug! That's how you change the world—one person at a time."

"Times are slowly changing. My niece is married to a white guy and Henry's daughter married a black guy. What used to be unaccepted is becoming more accepted, though the Reserves had more of a problem accepting us as a couple than our families did. Maybe that's because our families knew us as individuals and to the military we were just a white man and a black woman."

"It doesn't take much time in the South to realize that the confederacy is still around. Those flags are still flying. Most people in the Reserves haven't spent as much time in active duty in the military as Veronica and I have, so they're still stuck in some small-time attitudes. I've had white fellows say to me, 'You can take them to bed, but you can't bring them home.' Well that's just not my way of looking at things. And we have as good a marriage as anyone I know. I love this woman, I really do."

"I don't hold any grudge against anyone in Henry's family who held a grudge against me. I chalk it up to ignorance—fear of the unknown. I don't take it that personally. There was no way I was going to leave my husband because someone couldn't accept us as a couple, and I think his relatives came to respect that through the years. In my opinion, love always outweighs hate and will win out in the end. My own sister used to have a problem with Henry's race, but now she loves him to death. She'll value his opinion over mine. Like he said, the world is changed one person at a time."

"I keep our picture right behind my desk. When people walk in, the first thing they see after shaking my hand is that picture, and I say, 'Oh, that's me and my wife. She works right across the hall.' I love my work. People know when they have a problem, they can come to me and I'll help them out. I love

> "The hard part is letting go of the past while never forgetting history."

my wife, too. When it's time to go to lunch, she'll stick her head around the partition, and off we'll go! That doesn't mean that when we go into a restaurant together, people don't sometimes stare at us. We'll get to the point where we want to turn around and say, 'Hi! Do I know you?'"

"At this one restaurant, they didn't want to serve us..."

"...and I said 'Is this Denny's?' Then all of a sudden, they're like all over themselves to serve us!"

"Being here in Charleston just gives me chills. We're right around the corner from where the slave ships would come in and slaves were put on the auction block. It's a flea market now and I asked a black fellow who was working down there, 'How do you stand being in a place with such a terrible history?' and he says, 'You have to make a living and you have to let go of the past.'"

"The hard part is letting go of the past while never forgetting history," says Henry as he takes Veronica's hand.

1 was born in Gastonia, North Carolina in 1934 and from my earliest memory, I was ready to get out of there as soon as I could," says Bob, laughing. "It was a little cotton mill town, and I always hated it and told people I was from Charlotte. The draft for the Korean War was still in place when I graduated from high school. I decided if I had to be in the military, I might as well be an officer and a gentleman, so I went to the Citadel. Most of my educational experience was segregated, but outside of class I had quite a few black friends. I used to have a little illegal fireworks operation with a black buddy named Garbo and I used to love to head over to the black nightclub in Charlotte. Of course, back then I never dreamed of dating outside of my race, even though I was practically raised by the black woman who worked for my family. When Aunt Nanny retired, Dad built a house for her behind our house. Delphine raised my brother, and, as a little kid, he used to call her 'morphine'! The South back then was somehow segregated and yet integrated at the same time. It's almost impossible to explain to someone who didn't live through that period."

I had a different childhood in so many ways," says Kathy, "and not just because of the fifteen-year age difference between us. I grew up in Philadelphia, the youngest of twelve. My dad died when I was a baby, and my mom somehow held things together, though times were sometimes lean. My mother was a nurse, and most of her clients were white. Our public schools were integrated, and most of my friends were white because we were a twenty percent minority. My mother wouldn't allow me to date in high school, no matter what race a boy was! I went to Temple University, which was predominately white. Back in 1967, I was pretty much the only black person on campus, but I was so used to being a minority, that I wasn't uncomfortable about it. Our neighborhood in the fifties was integrated, and I don't remember experiencing much racism until we moved into a brownstone in Philly. As soon as we moved in, our white neighbors began moving out. We moved into a white neighborhood and it transformed into a black neighborhood. 'White flight' wasn't just theory,

we saw it firsthand. After I became an aerospace engineer, I had a hard time meeting black guys. First, there are very few black engineers, and if I met some guy at a bar on Friday night and told him I was a rocket scientist, the conversation was over before it started! I used to lie and say I was a secretary, just so they would hang around and talk to me."

"The only reason Kathy and I were able to get together as a couple," laughs Bob, who is an aerospace engineer himself, "is because she dummied herself down so much, I wasn't afraid of her!"

"We can laugh about it now, but it wasn't very funny being a black female scientist on a Saturday night. The worst part was, when I did meet a black guy, I'd stay in the relationship when it was obviously wrong, because there wasn't a whole lot to choose from. Bob was the first white

> "I could just imagine all my slave ancestors' bodies rising up out of the ground, saying 'How dare you! After all we've been through, you're moving to Alabama with a white man!'"

guy I ever got involved with romantically. After my divorce, I realized that I had to broaden my horizons if I was going to have male companionship."

"I never dated outside my race either, until Kathy, after my own divorce. She was my new co-worker at the Naval Research Lab, and I just liked everything about her. I honestly can't remember having a moment's hesitation about her race, or anything else about her, for that matter."

"It was pretty much of a whirlwind romance. We moved in together after a few months. I think his sister was pretty surprised when she first met me. Even though he didn't pay much attention to my race, she certainly noticed when we first met. It was pretty funny. I'll never forget her

expression when I stepped out of the car," chuckles Kathy. "The first thing that blurts out of her mouth is, 'Isn't she cute!'"

"She immediately got on the phone and told everyone in the family, so they wouldn't be shocked when they met Kathy."

"I fell in love with his mother the first time we talked on the phone. She's a very stately looking and sounding white woman, a lady in the very best sense of the word. My own large family runs the gamut of racial attitudes, from one sister who absolutely dislikes all whites on principle, to a brother who married a German woman. When someone in my family says something against whites, I say 'But Robert's white,' and they'll say 'But he's different.' Both races can somehow make racist assumptions at the same time they think those that they like of a different race are the exception. I think the more we know each other, the more we realize our similarities instead of our differences. Segregation leads to suspicion and hostility. My first trip down South in the early sixties, I was shocked to see

> "We moved into a white neighborhood and it transformed into a black neighborhood. 'White flight' wasn't just theory, we saw it first hand."

the 'colored' signs. I was used to sharing a Coke with my white schoolmates back in Pennsylvania and couldn't accept that I wouldn't be served a Coke because I was 'colored'!

"We had been happily living together outside of D.C. for years, and since neither one of us wanted kids, there wasn't any compelling reason to get married, until I got a job down at the missile center in Huntsville, Alabama and she had a job offer down there with NASA..."

"...and I said, 'The only way I'll ever live in Alabama is if we are married.' I could just imagine all my slave ancestors bodies rising up out of the ground, saying 'How dare you! After all we've been through, you're moving to Alabama with a white man!' I wanted to at least be married, so the neighbors

wouldn't look at me like some sort of concubine," laughs Kathy. "Seriously, though, I wanted to get married as a reassurance to us both that we were totally committed, even if our work sometimes kept us apart."

"The interesting thing is after all our trepidation about the Deep South, we found it a wonderful place to live. Everyone was really warm and friendly, and we didn't feel out of place at all. One of the few times we felt we were discriminated against was when we went to the justice of the peace to get married."

"He was downright rude to us," continues Kathy, with hurt in her voice from that stinging memory. "After we said our vows, he just turned his back on us and stormed out of the room without so much as a formal handshake or a token 'congratulations.' We just stood there looking at one another like we'd been slapped."

"I told her that it wasn't because of our different races but because she was so much younger than me, the old coot was jealous."

"Whatever his reason for being hostile, it hurt our feelings."

"That's true, but we were able to laugh about it and go on and have a good time. No matter what your situation is, you can't let other people's opinions wreck your happiness."

"The interesting thing is that even though Robert and I have only on rare occasion experienced discrimination because of being a mixed couple, I suspect that one reason we kind of stick to ourselves and don't socialize much is because we can't help but remember racist things our friends and family said before we were together. I admit, I'm probably more sensitive than Robert, but probably with good reason. The worst problem I have is with my black friends, who act like I'm some sort of traitor. I think folks should accept and respect love above and beyond color lines. Robert and I click as companions in a way that transcends race. When my white friends say, 'Kathy, you're not really black,' they don't realize that I don't particularly think that's a compliment. I'm the colored gal that you can bring home and feel good about yourself because you can say to yourself, 'See—I'm not racist!' One of the biggest changes in the past twenty years is that if a black marries a white, nowadays they're more welcome in the white community. Before the Civil Rights Movement in the early sixties, if blacks and whites mixed, they'd be more accepted in the black community.

Before integration, blacks were more accepting of people of all hues. Now there's more hostility towards whites."

"Kathy and I have both felt that our black friends are more racist than our white friends, though Kathy sometimes perceives things as racist that I don't pay any mind." Bob turns to her and says, "Remember when you were wearing that big straw hat on the boat?"

"And I was wearing my dark glasses, feeling like a glamorous movie star until your daughter teased me and said I looked like I should be picking cotton! A few days later , when I said I wanted to get the laundry started before we went out to eat, she said 'Dad, don't let her show up with a basket of laundry on her head.' Now I don't think I'm being paranoid, but she wasn't seeing me as an astrophysicist stepmother, all she could see was a cotton picking, laundry totin', love slave mistress! Her primary contact with blacks was domestic help, so that's how she saw me. The miracle of my relationship with Robert is that our mutual respect and love for each other has allowed us to rise above the prejudices of our backgrounds."

Developed and produced by

VERVE
EDITIONS

Burlington Vermont
www.verveeditions.com

Designed by

BIG
EYEDEA
VISUAL DESIGN

Waitsfield, Vermont
stacey@bigeyedea.com

DAFINA BOOKS are published by
Kensington Publishing Corp.
850 Third Avenue, New York, NY 10022

All Kensington titles, imprints and distributed lines are available at
special quantity discounts for bulk purchases for sales promotion,
premiums, fund-raising, educational or institutional use.

Special book excerpts or customized printings can also be created to
fit specific needs. For details, write or phone the office of the
Kensington Special Sales Manager: Kensington Publishing Corp.,
850 Third Avenue, New York, NY 10022,
Attn. Special Sales Department. Phone: 1-800-221-2647.

Dafina Books and the Dafina logo Reg. U.S. Pat. & TM Off.

Library of Congress Card Catalog Number: 2002101739
ISBN 0-7582-0207-5

First Printing: October 2002
10 9 8 7 6 5 4 3 2 1

Printed in the Hong Kong

ACKNOWLEDGEMENTS

A heartfelt "thank you" to all the couples in this book, whose love and respect for each other transcend the lingering legacy of slavery and whose children blur the final boundaries of segregation. Once again, I'm grateful to have the unwavering support of my book packager, Gary Chassman of Verve Editions, whose belief in this project has made it a reality. I'm also fortunate to have Stacey Hood as the designer of *Love in Black & White*. Working with the two of them makes work a pleasure. I'm grateful that Dafina's Karen Thomas saw the need for a book like this to exist and appreciate Kathleen Friestad's careful line edit of the manuscript.